THE
WIDOW STIGMA

Alisha Robbins

MAPLE
PUBLISHERS

The Widow Stigma

Author: Alisha Robbins

Copyright © Alisha Robbins (2024)

The right of Alisha Robbins to be identified as author of this work has been asserted by the author in accordance with section 77 and 78 of the Copyright, Designs and Patents Act 1988.

First Published in 2024

ISBN 978-1-915796-99-8 (Paperback)
       978-1-915996-00-8 (eBook)

Book cover design and book layout by:

    White Magic Studios
    www.whitemagicstudios.co.uk

Published by:

    Maple Publishers
    Fairbourne Drive, Atterbury,
    Milton Keynes,
    MK10 9RG, UK
    www.maplepublishers.com

"You give yourself space to grow when you understand that you don't need to be present everywhere"

-MOHIT PANCHAL

"A time will come in your life when some people will regret why they treated you wrong"

INTRODUCTION

The story tells of the compelling journey of a young British-born woman whose parents arrange a marriage and send her to live in a strange country. Upon arrival, Andromeda is forced to adapt to the customary practices and adhere to the rigid expectations of her in laws.

The challenges of a wife a widow and a single parent are all laid bare in this evocative, heart-rending narrative.

A story that speaks of duelling families, cultural disparities, and two worlds that could not have been any more different. At the heart of the conflict, lies the life of a young woman who had to adapt to her surroundings without question, to appease her in-laws.

From the naive girl, whose innocence and sanity are taken to the extreme she is transformed into a woman with a single purpose. Her mission, becomes a quest of survival, from the maelstrom that threatens the very fabric of her and that of her children's existence.

Brief Back Story of Marriage

Andromeda was still in the throes of childhood, before her parents received a marriage proposal for their daughter from Pakistan. Although Andromeda was only 15 years old, she was still at school although it was now her last year. They would be finishing after the exams. Andromeda hoped to go to college after school as all her friends were also going once they had taken and passed their exams. The prospect was, too great an opportunity to pass up. Proposals like these were few and far between. There were many families who would undoubtedly jump at the chance for their daughters to receive such a wonderful proposal.

Andromeda's parents had promptly taken up the offer without further ado. They had registered their agreement without a moment's notice and began putting all the necessary arrangements into place for their daughter's marriage. It was of little relevance that Andromeda had never met the man she was supposed to marry. The fact that they were second distant cousins and near relations was enough to guarantee that the match would be a good one for their daughter.

In time, Andromeda simply had to agree and accept her parent's decision. It was for the best. She had to get married someday, her parents reasoned, good proposals were hard to come by and they did not intend to sit on their hands and wait for the next one. Their minds were made up.

Andromeda knew next to nothing about him except for the fact that he was a distant cousin. He was well-educated and had a promising career in the military, what more could they have asked for in a good match for their daughter? He seemed to tick all the right boxes. A military man of distinction who in his officer's uniform accorded unequivocal respect and commanded authority wherever he went. She could sense her parent's unconcealed pride at the thought of their daughter entering such a prestigious match. They had been exuberant with joy when the first letter containing the proposal had arrived.

It had been a rather unobtrusive encounter at the airport in which both parties had met for the first time and n~

knew anything about the other apart from the names. "A match made in the dark" thought Andromeda cynically.

Letters and telegrams were the most popular mode of communication and the house phone. Face time and video calling had not arrived as yet. Now it was the main form of communication with people across the digital divide, spanning continents and remote regions, bringing people closer than ever before. The world had shrunk considerably.

Andromeda wondered if she had had the luxury of video calling then maybe she would have had a better idea and a clear picture of the man she was being betrothed to. That would have helped her to decide before being taken to Pakistan whether she still wanted to marry him or not, she reasoned.

A month later a hasty, engagement had taken place while Andromeda was in the UK. Upon arrival in Pakistan, she met the man chosen for her, when they arrived at the bustling airport of Islamabad. She remembered the first day when they had met. It had been an unobtrusive encounter at the airport in which both parties had met for the first time and neither knew anything about the other apart from their names and the family connection "A match made in the dark" Andromeda had thought cynically

They had greeted each other cordially and with a semblance of diplomacy in their shy mannerisms. He was not so tall, but average and quite skinny, she had thought, deeply tanned from having spent a lot of time in the searing and scorching heat of the country no doubt. He was clean-shaven, with brown eyes, black hair, and nothing remarkable in his features, except the smile that lit up his intelligent eyes, when he introduced himself to his bride-to-be.

He exuded warmth towards Andromeda and her father as he welcomed them both. He had nice smooth hands she noted in a glance, long slender fingers, tapered like a pianist, with clean cut nails. That was something at least she thought sardonically. He seemed personable she had thought and well-groomed in the way he spoke and offered them refreshments and escorted them to their rooms once they had arrived at their hotel. No doubt it was the gruelling training he had received in the military that exacted only the best from its officers, she thought. He walked with a smooth self-assured gait, brimming with confidence and an aura of uprightness that commanded instant respect from his juniors.

After a few days of rest, things had moved with rapid motion as Andromeda and her father set off with her fiancée to make the long journey to her husband's ancestral village in the Punjab.

The village was located on the rural remote outskirts of the Punjab village district of Sanghoi, a village and union council of Jhelum. This was situated in the Punjab province of Pakistan.

A few weeks later, a flurry of wedding preparations, followed. Days of celebration preceded the ostentatious marriage ceremony, rituals, and traditions, which Andromeda was alien to and found fascinatingly bizarre.

Andromeda's father returned to the UK having fulfilled his paternal duty. She had always been his favourite child, being the first of her 4 siblings, and he knew that one day she would get married, except no one had told him that it would be the most difficult thing he would ever have to experience. That day had arrived a lot sooner than expected. His beloved daughter, his first born now belonged to another family and he hoped and prayed fervently as the silent tears trickled down his eyes, that his son-in-law would take good care of his precious daughter and protect her always. She would live a life of ease and contentment and would want for nothing he assured himself.

PROLOGUE

Left to cope and adjust to her new life by herself amid hostile relatives, Andromeda had found herself at odds with everyone in her new family and the extended pool of relatives she met. The strong sense of discord and seething resentment alarmed her as did the never-ending family politics and conflicts which raged on needlessly.

Over time the conflicts had risen unabated to such magnitudes that her marriage teetered on the brink of collapse. Despite the huge cultural differences and the hostile environment she finds herself in, Andromeda manages to hold on by the last tendrils of her resistance.

Following the sudden demise of her husband, Andromeda finds herself openly castigated by her in-laws and relations. Throughout her marriage, their antics and continued chastisement had eroded her self-esteem.

Despite their continued efforts to undermine her, she had remained unperturbed and unyielding which had only served to inflame tensions further.

They were clever to disguise their antics in her husband's presence. He never suspected anything and neither did Andromeda tell him. She knew how close he was to his family, and would be less inclined to believe her anyway. She was just a silly immature girl to them including her husband. Nothing Andromeda did or said could be taken seriously. She had had to grow up very fast, from the moment she became a wife and a mother, but that did not endear her any more to her in-laws. They had to find fault in every single thing she did. Nobody took her seriously until it got to the point that she began to doubt herself too.

The continued barrage of criticism always seemed to find its mark leaving Andromeda floundering in a void of uncertainty and insecurities. Why did they dislike her so much? She bemoaned inwardly. However in front of her husband they behaved in a civil fashion towards her almost lauding her efforts to fit in, giving her undue praise so that her husband did not suspect anything out of the ordinary. He beamed with gratitude and joy to watch his family welcome his young wife into their midst. Beneath the surface of plastered smiles and displays of warmth lurked more sinister intentions.

Under their cunning guise of looking out for her, they managed to convince her husband that they were on her side and they could do no wrong in his eyes. Yet the moment she was left alone with them, the outwardly pleasant demeanour turned to one of malignant disgust. Oblivious to the hurt and pain they caused by the callousness of their actions they set her to work, all the while jeering and mocking at her ineptitude. Her silence and submissiveness only emboldened them more.

As far as they were concerned, she was a useless, stupid girl with not a single working brain cell. She came from humble beginnings and knew nothing about their culture. This made her a prime target for harassment. What on earth did their brother see in her? The fact that she was a British born girl did not impress them so much, she was a total misfit amongst them. She was clueless about life and the customs in Pakistan.

Following the sudden death of her husband, 16 years later Andromeda finds herself navigating the turbulent waters of widowhood. She finds herself cast as a stigma amongst her kind, a woman, shirked by her peers, a woman to be avoided, lest her bad luck affect those who come into proximity with her. The younger women, of marriageable age would stop mingling with her, and avoid her altogether. They did not want to be tainted by her bad luck. A widow was exactly that, a product of some curse sent down, she was considered bad luck. The thread of superstition was rife amongst Andromeda's relatives and ran like a loose thread unravelling doubts and creating fear in everyone's minds.

It was not long before everyone had ghosted her. Wherever she turned, she was met with a cold wall of frigid silence, an imperceptible show of disunity towards her. Those who had once displayed civility towards her and had gladly welcomed her into their inner circles were now shunning her openly without any compunction.

Andromeda discovers her newly acquired status as a widow and brings her present life to a whole new debilitating level. She feels humiliation and a deep sense of sudden abandonment. Looking around her, casting her eyes for a single friend, she finds nobody she can trust or rely upon. They had all forsaken her.

She was all alone now.

Young widows if lucky and open to remarrying, were supported by their families and could get remarried and start their lives anew. In worst cases, opportunistic men would prey on such widows, to divulge them of potential assets, inheritance, and whatever worldly possessions of value they may have inherited from their late husbands.

She had heard countless tales of widows who had been marginalised and reduced to insignificance. To find herself in the same situation was hard to grasp let alone believe. This was made worse by having to experience the changes in the way people treated her.

Upon arrival, Andromeda's first impression of the country was the gender disparity. Women were deemed to be inferior to men and had very little say and control in everyday affairs. This was more apparent in her husband's family.

The menacing presence and harsh tone of patriarchal command hung in the air like an invisible smog, clouding judgments and resisting reason. Andromeda would go on to discover on that just by voicing an opinion or eliciting a suggestion for that matter would never go down well with her in laws. They would undermine her at every juncture. To her detriment she had attempted a few times to warrant a suggestion or speak her mind when she felt like she was being attacked, this had only served to unleash their wrath.

Like a pack of hungry predators, they had descended upon her head, raining down curses and jibes, and putting her effectively in her place. She had no standing or position in the family home except to keep her mouth shut and follow orders. As an outsider and a daughter in law, they would not tolerate any individual opinion or back chat from her, for if she dared, they would snuff her out with one swift, sharp rebuke. Her husband could not complain or protest as he had been raised in a house where patriarchy was a given, and to assume the position of the head of the household, giving in or submitting to a wife was not in their practiced code of rules.

It was the men who held the supreme positions and entitlement to all decisions in the household. To speak as an equal, and offer decisions invited scorn and indifference, so it was better to remain quiet and submit to the men's wishes.

Her in-laws ensured that she did not stand a chance in the first place, married or not, being treated on an equal footing was unheard of. The sheer level of misogyny Andromeda had encountered was staggering.

Unfortunately for Andromeda that progress had not reached her in- laws and the culture she was now embedded in. The village seemed to be cut off from the civilised world in terms of advancement and literacy as well as geographically isolated from the bigger cities and towns, where some modicum of advancement could be found.

Alongside patriarchy, matriarchy existed in the guise of her mother in-law and sisters-in-law. Their word was law and sandwiched between the two oppressive schools of thought. Her odds at defending herself were increased significantly, following her husband's death Andromeda, finds herself shunned wherever she goes.

Feeling like a branded heretic, she can feel the lynching mobs drawing near, ready to launch themselves upon her, their talons drawn, blood thirsty eyes, boring into her with their unmistakable intent and they began advancing upon her steadily with deadly intent. She has nowhere to go, nowhere to hide, no-one to turn to.

They see her as some sort of witch conjuring spells, and wreaking bad luck down upon them. The inhumane screams grow louder, animal like in their intensity until she realises they are coming from her, all kinds of horrors manifest, in her mind. Seeing the bloodthirsty crowds draw nearer closing in on her, not unlike the witches of a long forgotten past, she too is being pulled, and pushed to stand trial by the raging torrential river, before they strap her tightly to a chair ready for the dunking. She is fading, her lifeless body hangs between the living and the dead. At that moment her eyes shoot open, looking around panic stricken as she gets her bearings.

She sits up in bed drenched with perspiration clutching the covers tighter around her and sobbed. It had been another nightmare as the sharp shaft of light filtering in from the half closed curtain blinded her, she felt the throes of a migraine lingering on the edge, migraine that would unleash its fury and last three days at least. She winced in pain as a stabbing knife like pain coursed through her head. It was all stress she knew, as more was being piled on every day at the thought of how she was going to manage. She had to compose her scattered thoughts and get a hold of herself, she told herself angrily. Help was not coming anytime soon she was alone and had to get used to the fact very soon, whether she liked it or not.

The nightmares were becoming frequent by the day. It did not help matters when the other wives in the compound where they lived were antagonistic towards her. Once they had been the epitome of neighbourly kindness and hospitality. Now they openly glared at her and made a hasty departure when they saw her coming. Those that Andromeda did run into barely stopped to ask how she was coping, and muttered a quick greeting, rushing off on the pretext that they had to be somewhere. They could not even bring themselves to meet her eye as they did so.

Some would cross over to the other path to avoid any encounter and need for conversation, or simply look the other way. She had become a contagion, to be avoided, lest she infect others with her incurable disease.

Would it have appeased their conscience had she dutifully burned in the funeral pyre as a sati or drowned in the sea with weights attached to her ankles, she thought sardonically.

She had been reduced to a mere caricature of herself, nothing short of being buried alive alongside her husband, given their smug satisfaction, and sidelong glances at each other. She was a living, breathing corpse.

She hoped and prayed that she was not about to become another statistic, a victim of mind-sets, frozen in the time-warped attitudes and crushed by illiteracy by the very people "who" were supposed to protect her.

CHAPTER 1

FOREBODING BEIJING 2000

He had only been gone for two weeks but it had seemed much longer than that. Her gut was screaming at her that something calamitous was about to happen, That sense of foreboding, the awareness of heightened senses telling her, screaming at her that something terrible was going to happen, dark menacing clouds of trepidation were making their way across the chaotic mess of thoughts that were swirling like dancing phantoms in her head, mocking her, taunting her.

A heavy sense of impending horror clung to the air like a stubborn odour, refusing to dissipate. It gnawed away at her senses.

Her gut was twisting and turning flipping over, as if it was trying to tell her something, and she simply did not want to know. That night she turned up the thermostat one degree more, the flat was warm enough but she felt a chill that ran through to her bones.

It was December after all, the wintry month had brought sleet and snow spells, outside the tops of the trees, and houses dotted about were coated with a white velvety blanket of snow. The cars parked below the 15-storey flat where she lived looked like little white ringed seals slumbering beneath their white covers.

Although the flat was, small, but it was adequate for her family. It was quite warm and well-insulated from the cold.

The owners had ensured that everything was in place and full working order.

Andromeda had rented it for the year. Her husband's posting had come to an end, and they were due to go back home to Pakistan once he returned from his trip to the UK. She had balked at the thought of going back to the same situation she had left 3 years ago, the interminable, fights, arguments, conflicts, the unhappiness of trying and failing to be accepted by his family.

More years of parrying to their whims and serving them awaited her. Even after 12 years, she was no closer to attaining a truce with her in-laws. They were simply worlds apart.

Now her children were growing and getting wiser, she could not subject them to all the family drama. It was unhealthy and damaging to her children's development. To see their parents fighting and squabbling over infallible matters was the last thing she wanted for them. They had already seen too much, in their earlier years, and it was damaging for their development if things continued in the same fashion.

Her in-laws were never going change no matter what she did. She could bend over backward like a contortionist, doing the impossible, but to little effect, they would still attempt to break her down until she was nothing.

In the end she had managed to convince her husband that she wanted to stay on in China and that he could return to Pakistan and continue his job. She could work in the school as a Montessori teacher in Beijing, where she had already completed a 12 month contract. It would be a small price to pay to have another year of peace and calm before she went back. Reluctantly he had agreed. She had noted with surprise and concern that he had been quiet and pensive of late.

His compliance in letting her stay came as a shock, as she did not expect him to cave in so quickly. Perhaps he had other things on his mind, his career, the move, the upcoming travel to the UK as short as it was, who knew?

He rarely let Andromeda have an insight into the inner trappings of his mind, even though she was his wife, but the distance between them lay like an invisible shroud, masking their true feelings from each other. Marriage had seemed to have lost its lustre a long time ago, Andromeda thought sadly, as they seemed to have just been going through the motions lately.

As the night grew darker and the shadows, danced and flitted on the walls, that sinking feeling was growing heavier and despondent. They were taunting her as if they knew what was headed her way, yet she herself could not put her finger on it.

She lay in her bed tossing and turning, trying to banish the feelings of growing unease, sleep was evading her too. Her husband was due back home in a few days.

The children could barely contain themselves, chattering away animatedly, they laughed and played and fought as siblings did. Rejoicing at the thought that papa would be home very soon, bringing with him lots of gifts they couldn't wait for tomorrow to come.

* * *

CHAPTER 2

THE NIGHTMARE WARNING

One of her closest friends, Sophia, lived on the storey below them in the 16-storey apartment. She had planned to spend the evening at Andromeda's home.

She was a heavy set woman, pleasant looking face, and a sweet smile. Although younger than Andromeda, she looked worn for her years, the pounds had piled up on her and she struggled at times to walk, due to her large heft and size.

She was an amazing, wife, and mother, as well as a dutiful daughter in law. Both her in-laws lived with her and her 5 children, she never had a moment's respite from housework.

Sophia often vented to Andromeda about her disgruntled in laws who had it so easy living in relative comfort with a caring dutiful daughter in law to care for their needs, but they were never shy of telling Sophia the opposite.

She had amazing patience and tolerance, Andromeda thought to persevere as she did. She guessed that in-laws of such mentality were a prevailing theme throughout her culture. Sophia loved to cook and much to Andromeda's shame whose own cooking was limited to a few dishes, sampled many of her friend's culinary offerings almost daily.

She possessed a pleasant demeanour, soft spoken, compassionate, and caring to a fault. Sophia endeared herself to everyone she met. Andromeda was no exception. Both women had grown closer over time and had known one another for years and were very close like sisters, they had no secrets and shared many things without trepidation. No doubt they would be up all night talking into the early hours.

It was lovely for Andromeda to have such a warm caring friend who knew her like nobody else. They had met in Beijing where both their families had been posted for 4 years.

There were many other families in the diplomatic corps they came to know quite well. She liked Sophia, and they had both clicked right from the start. They understood one another quite well and before they knew it, they had become the best of friends and confidantes to one another. It was comforting for Andromeda to have a friend with whom she could share and vent her frustrations with and the same applied to Sophia.

They both lifted one another's spirits and it was a lovely feeling Andromeda thought, particularly as she had had no close friends back home to share the fun times with. Living in a joint family system in which her in-laws continuously lived with her all throughout the year alternating between themselves as someone also had to stay back in the village to manage the affairs of their lands.

Andromeda was constantly up to her elbows in household duties, catering to everyone's whims. With an exhausted sigh of relief she went to bed each night knowing that she had to wake up early before her mother in law who rose very early. Andromeda had to make sure she had prepared breakfast before the different breakfast shifts began in succession. Her sister in laws with their children and husbands would wakeup mid-morning and by the time Andromeda had finished serving everyone it would be time to start preparing for the midday meal. It was never ending. In all the chaos of these mornings her husband would get up and get ready for work, he would ask for a continental style breakfast as opposed to the traditional fare his family were accustomed to 'parathas' (buttery crepes and fried egg or sometimes an omelette.)

He seemed completely oblivious to his wife's flustered state having to run around all day along attending to his family and their children. She could not complain for he would take affront to her pleas of exhaustion. She was there to take care of his family and he wanted to hear no more, she was duty bound as his wife, she had to obey her husband and at the same time please his family. Andromeda's pleas were thus silenced in the face of her husband's patriarchal stance. She had no choice but to obey.

They had argued and fought constantly but he had remained resolute and tight lipped throughout He would not hear a single word about his family. In his eyes they could not do wrong and thus so it continued. He refused to waver from his stance. It had been an unpleasant time of marital discord Andromeda remembered with sadness.

Here in China it had been a total contrast. She had never felt so alive and welcomed with gusto the liberating feeling that accompanied her the moment they had flown out as a family to embark upon their 4 year posting. Like a bird that had been caged for too long in captivity she felt her wings unfurl gradually before one final push and she was soaring beyond the clouds up and up. Her chest bursting with the song and cheer. She was free at last.

Meeting Sophie, she had realised that they both had a lot in common which had forged their connection immeasurably. It was good to know that she was not alone with the problems she had encountered as a young woman living in a joint family system. There were many out there in her situation, some suffering far worse than herself. She should count her blessings and be grateful that she got to travel places with her husband. Some women barely ever left their villages and ended up spending their entire lives in one place ultimately ending up with being buried there. With this she shivered, quickly dispelling the thought and admonishing herself, yes she was lucky in some respects.

Their husbands also shared a mutual profound respect for each other. Sophie had 5 children, who studied alongside Andromeda's children, so it was always fun to have family gatherings and host events together. Sophia's husband was a Professor of Science, who taught 8 and 9 graders at the international school for expatriate families.

Andromeda could not have been any happier. She knew a lot of people and having attended infinite parties and receptions not to mention the gatherings at the homes of diplomat wives, it was an endless swirl of invitations, and she had at least Sophia, the one friend she could count on always.

Although it was cold and freezing outside, the temperature was warm inside the cosy flat.

Andromeda slept with the ceiling fans on all through the year. It was the white noise that induced her to sleep better she had found.

She gazed at the ceiling as they hummed overhead like giant whirling dervishes pushing the air around the rooms, her friend could not suppress a shudder, as she wrapped her cotton shawl tightly around her.

Andromeda could also feel a chill creeping up into her bones, although they were in the middle of summer, and the mercury sat at a comfortable 24 degrees. They had talked for hours late into the early morning when the first light of dawn had begun to appear.

* * *

CHAPTER 3

THE LAST GOODBYE

It was the night before news of his sudden death arrived, she had dreamt an uneasy dream that belied her worst fears and he had called her one last time. Had he also received some kind of premonition?

It was then that the shrill tone of the phone rang out piercing the quiet night air and alarming Andromeda from her stupor.

He seemed flustered, she detected a rising note of agitation in his voice as he questioned his wife repeatedly, if she was okay, had she been ill? Were the children OK? Had anything happened that she was not telling him? Was someone ill? He sounded agitated as he spoke. A voice tinged with heavy concern and perhaps sadness she sensed. He did not seem like his usual talkative self. Normally he always had a lot to say.

Despite his wife's repeated reassurances, he was not convinced. He went on to relay the vivid dream that he had. He had seen Andromeda alone and visibly distressed and this had disturbed him greatly and woken him up the night before. It was as if he had also sensed something was coming but not quite sure. He had felt uneasy for the past few days but did not want to worry his wife needlessly. He could not shake off the feeling of impending doom. Although he would be reunited with his family tomorrow, something prompted him to call and check on Andromeda and the children. He realised the lateness of the hour, but he had to hear her voice and know that she and their children were ok.

This was why he had been prompted to call her at this ungodly hour fearing the worst. After a few reassurances and placatory words, they said goodbye and hung up.

Andromeda wondered to herself, what exactly had he seen? He was holding back. However, she wanted to allay his concerns and laughingly chastised him for the lateness of the hour, it was 2 a.m. that morning, and he was supposed to be catching an Aeroflot flight from London to Beijing in a few hours. Then they would all be together again. She had missed him terribly as had the children. Although it had only been a couple of weeks, he had gone away longer for months at a time during sea trials. Somehow this felt different.

The kids had missed him. Andromeda was a good attentive mother, but the children were very attached to their father and had missed him terribly, they had been counting down the days of his arrival with unrestrained excitement.
She reassured her husband that all was fine and that in the next 9 hours they would see each other. The children were very excited of course and she had managed to get them to sleep with great difficulty, especially the little one, who was a miniature force of energy to reckon with. Eventually he too had managed to drift off to sleep hours later nestled in the crook of his older brother' s arm on the single bed they shared, whilst the girls slept on the adjacent one, contented, and flustered by the day's playful activities.

Andromeda paused in her cleaning up the mess in the room to stare down adoringly at her sleeping children as, their soft snores filtered through the room, away in their own little dream worlds. She bent down to kiss each of them, being careful not to wake them, and turned to switch off the light and gently close the door.

They had been so excited that papa was home going to be home soon that, Andromeda faced an uphill task getting her children settled in for the night.

Their excitement was beyond measure on seeing their father again. It had seemed like he had gone forever. Tomorrow they would be regaling their father with endless accounts and news of all that he had missed with an endless litany of complaints no doubt.

She sighed as she bent to pick up the little cars and toys strewn across the floor. Her 3-year old, Elijah was notorious for keeping everybody on their toes, was like a little tornado running around all day, weaving in and out of curtains and hiding places, much to the delight of his older siblings. Being the baby of the family Elijah was coddled and spoilt by all especially his father whose presence he had also sorely missed in these last two weeks.

He babbled incoherently with a few strung out sentences sparking laughter with his antics, but Andromeda could tell he missed his papa often watching him looking pensive and forlorn at times sitting wistfully in the window seat staring down at the noisy scenes unfurling below, the heady lines of traffic coiling and merging like metallic snakes between the carts and bikes and throngs of people.

His older brother Samuel was very close to him so he often kept a watchful adoring eye on his little brother coaxing him out of corners and hiding places to play games with him. Elijah traipsed around on his little wobbly legs following his brother everywhere he went. They two were inseparable.

The girls occupied themselves, preening over their girlish possessions, and often joining with their brothers so the flat resonated with their shrieks and screams sometimes erupting in arguments that flared up with regular frequency. One minute they would be engaged in normal chatter, and a few moments later, they would be squabbling over nothing.

* * *

CHAPTER 4

THE MESSAGE

Lately her husband's behaviour had been strange to say the least. A day earlier he had sent them a one line sentence in an e mail on the old school monitor and computer they had.

Andromeda's son who was 15 had beckoned frantically to his mother, a note of urgency and surprise in his voice. She remembered with sad vivid clarity, even anger at her husband why he would write such an abominable thing. There was no reason to frighten them all like this. She was furious at her husband.

They had gathered in her son's bedroom of their small flat huddled around the ageing monitor screen, her young one clamouring for attention, weaving in and out of their legs, one chubby hand clutching his favourite dinky car, as his mother and brother stood imperviously, with eyes transfixed on the computer. He remained blissfully unaware to the palpable tension that had now crept into the room. How wonderful it was to be so innocent and oblivious to the stresses and worries that being grown up entailed she thought.

Deep seated concern was etched upon Andromeda and her son's faces as they stared uncomprehendingly at the monitor which flickered and cast its pale bluish translucent glow illuminating their faces.

Then there it was, as she felt a chill shoot right through to her bones. Two words had stood out on the flickering monitor, a dark contrast, to the pale washed blue, capitalised, and leaving no doubt to its menacing message.

I'M DEAD!

* * *

CHAPTER 5

PAPA IS COMING HOME

Only the whirr of the overhead fan and the shrieks of laughter of her two-year old penetrated the silence that fell between mother and son who looked at one another askance, questioning, puzzled confusion in their expression. Her son broke the silence first and spoke, "But Mum why?" Looking at Andromeda with down cast eyes, mouth upturned in bewilderment. "What does papa mean by this? Is he ok Mum? Why would he write this?"

Samuel was a clever boy, and far more mature than his 15 years. Compared to most boys his age, Andromeda observed that her son was hyper sensitive to even the smallest nuance of emotion and expression. He was like a vault of secrets with many layers of impenetrable steel.
Her son tucked away his emotions in the inner deepest recesses of his little soul. An over thinker, a worrier, sensitive by nature, he was what many would describe as an introvert, hard to read and often harder to reach when he turned inwardly any emotions that he may be feeling. She looked down into her son's upturned, questioning face, etched with grave concern.

She ruffled his hair fondly, placing her hand gently on his shoulder. She could feel the protruding ridge of his limbs. He was a skinny boy, no matter how much she tried to feed him, he was still in the midst of a growth spurt as adolescent changes were taking place. She looked into his eyes, two pools of liquid brown displaying sadness and incomprehension at his father's choice of words, and told him not to worry.

Her boy was growing up fast. He was her first born and Andromeda had a special place in her heart for him. She comforted her son, smiling at him and reassuring him that it was perhaps something his father had written as a joke and that he should not worry. Father would be back tomorrow and they could ask him then. She was sure there was a simple plausible excuse behind this.

Somewhat placated, her son offered up a reassuring smile at his mother, hugged her and then wandered off to join his exuberant siblings, who were now having a cushion fight in the small living room, shrieking with laughter and giggling uncontrollably, blissfully unaware and happy in their little world. Although she was phasing out the background noises in her mind, she could hear the chuckling and gurgling of her young one, impervious to his mother's concern.

It broke through her train of her thought as she looked down at him, clutching his favourite red dinky car and asking to be picked up. She picked him up, overcome with love at his incongruent chatter. He was hungry so she kissed him, put him down and walked to the kitchen to fix the children a snack. They were always wanting something to snack on, then, again, the energy they consumed all day long more than accounted for it. For the moment she was distracted as she busied herself getting the ingredients together.

The children were like jumping jacks, bounding about the small flat excitedly. They were full of beans, she could have done with some of their abundant energy herself. In between their exhaustive diplomatic functions, and dinner hosting parties at home as well as attending to the numerous events of their own delegation, Andromeda was exhausted. She just about managed to take care of the home and the children. She felt a pang of sadness that she could not spend as many hours with them as she liked. Although this was a prize posting, no doubt, but she had not expected the sheer volume of social obligations, which meant leaving her children every day with their maid.

* * *

CHAPTER 6

BEIJING

As she busied herself tidying up the flat. Her mind was racing. She had so much to do before tomorrow. Preparations to make, the fridge to restock and decide what's he was going to cook. Although now she had become quite proficient at managing multiple tasks and planning thanks to the 3 years they had spent in China. Where had the years gone? Time had flown by so fast she could not believe their posting had ended.

When they had first arrived, it was the year 2001. They had not known what to expect. It was a new country but also a new beginning for Andromeda. China was imply one of the most amazing countries she had ever visited. Not that she had visited many, but it was a fascinating Pandora's Box of wonders, waiting to be discovered by her.

Her husband had briefed her as to what was to be expected of her during their 3-year tenure in Beijing. After timetabling their commitments, and detailing the list of functions requiring their attendance, Andromeda knew she would be rushed off her feet without a moment to draw breath. The job came first. The diplomatic mission was of utmost importance and nothing else could supersede that.

Like many households who had arrived before and after them, they had been provided with a live-in housekeeper who foresaw the management of the home and the children during their tenure. She was vetted and trained in housekeeping, which reassured Andromeda.

Mai Lin had been amazing and the children loved her, despite the huge language gap. Mandarin was not an easy language to master.

Even though they had all picked up some fragments of it. Somehow they had all managed to understand each other which was more important. The children had picked up more Cantonese words than Andromeda and could speak full sentences with ease.

Mao Lin in turn, was a gentle, no nonsense. Middle-aged woman, loved the children and brought a lot of joy to their home.

As the tenure had ended, Andromeda had managed to persuade her husband to rent a flat, where she would live with her children and work as a sub English teacher at the Beijing Montessori School which was owned by an enterprising American woman. Andromeda had met Christina at a function and both had hit it off, resulting in Andromeda receiving a job offer which she was happy to take up.

It was not going to be easy, but it was a far better alternative to returning back to Pakistan, back into the thick of unrelenting conflicts which awaited her. She doubted very much that her in-laws would have mellowed in all this time. A leopard did not change his spots overnight she thought remembering the old cliche as was the likelihood of going home to the welcoming arms of her in-laws. It was unthinkable. Doubtless they would warm to her anytime soon, given the last 11 years in close confinement with them. They just tolerated her for the sake of their brother and son.

In all that time she had barely dented the surface of their steel clad exteriors to gain entry to their hearts and minds. It was a mission of futility she had thought to herself, letting out a slow drawn out breath of resignation. As the days grew closer to their return she grew more despondent knowing what awaited her back home, back in the fold of her husband's family. It did not look promising.

With a sigh Andromeda roused herself from her thoughts and focused back to the task at hand.

The laundry basket was spilling over with clothes, as she bent to retrieve discarded clothing and stuff them into the overflowing basket by the bathroom. She reminded herself to put the laundry on tomorrow. She was already behind, with the housework as clothes were strewn everywhere in the cluttered bathroom. She was constantly having to bend down and retrieve clothes and toys all day long that in itself it classed as a workout. Why her children could not put things into the baskets she painstakingly set up at intervals around the flat to keep it tidy

There were wrappers littered about, which she busied herself collecting She needed to cut down on their sugar consumption, especially sweets and chocolates.

She assembled the ingredients from the fridge, a medley of colourful fresh vegetables which she preceded to chop finely. She was making wraps tonight.

Sophie would pop in later tonight after she finished feeding her kids. The two friends could unwind and drink coffee together. It was almost 6.00, where had the day gone? She never liked the cold dark winter months. The days were far shorter to get much done aside from the fact that it filled her with terror, at how fast life was passing them by. Like a blink of an eye. There was so much she still wanted to do, but with 4 growing children, she would have to put her own hobbies and interests aside until each of them were independent enough to branch out on their own.

She placed the chicken fillets onto the grill pan after seasoning them. They would be served up in the tortilla wraps along with the freshly cut salad and mayonnaise. The children loved these, and could have them every day if they had their own way. Her mind drifted once again to her husband's bizarre message. At this point the chilling message with its millions of connotations had left no room for doubt as to its meaning.

What on earth could her husband mean? Why on earth would he write that? And what was he thinking? Sending such a dark and knowingly hurting message for his children to see? They were counting down the days to see their papa as they called him and he had to go and write this of all things. Really?

She was baffled and quite annoyed at her husband for pulling such a stunt. It angered her that he would put something out there, knowing it would cause his children anguish and alarm, the older ones in particular.

If he was in some kind of trouble, she could not imagine what, it was for the life of her. He would tell her she was sure of it.

They would be having words she thought determinedly once he was back. Perhaps he had some fallout with his family, that was not an impossibility, she thought wryly. His mother and brother had a penchant for inciting family drama and having witnessed their multiple acts of subterfuge and violations that had rocked the family's peace and stability, in particular her own marriage, she would not be surprised in the least if something had happened to inflame her husband.

What had triggered him to write that? Leaving her guessing and trying to come up with the answers was so unfair and uncouth of him, she thought angrily. She was his wife, the mother of his children, surely, he could share with her what was troubling him, what was going on in his mind to write a cryptic message and not elaborate.

Had he lost his mind? This and other questions flooded through her head. He was coming back tomorrow so why the need for the theatrics? If it was a joke it was a very sinister one and not in the least bit funny, she thought, bemused. Maybe he had, had some kind of disagreement with his brother and mother.

That would not surprise her she thought wryly. In house fighting and bickering over the smallest of things was commonplace within her husband's family. They argued for the sake of arguing. Sometimes it could get nasty and they would not talk to each other for years and just as suddenly reconcile again as if nothing happened.

Although most of those arguments were aimed at her as they tried to convince her husband, how useless she was, droning on about her ineptitude, and immaturity as a wife and sister in law. Except for the fact that this time she could not possibly be the cause. Back home they had plotted from the beginning to bring her down, one way or the other. There had been talk of getting her husband to leave her and remarry.

This time they would find him a better and a more suitable match. Andromeda had turned out to be a huge disappointment and a failure as far as they were concerned. They would not be making the same mistake twice. That was for sure. There were many willing ladies ready to take her place she knew with dismay. No-one cared in the least that he was already married and a father of 4 children, he was by far the most eligible man around who deserved to be happy than with that useless fool hardy wife of his they thought scornfully.

Andromeda knew she had to fight harder to save her marriage and she was confident that once her husband returned, from tomorrow, she would surprise him. Already she had learnt many things, from cooking to diplomacy skills and a lot more that no doubt would leave her husband impressed He would not want to look elsewhere she would exercise all her womanly wiles and powers to win back his heart. In due course his family would also finally begin to accept her.

She would see him tomorrow evening and come to learn more from her husband what had ensued there, and perhaps they would get to the bottom of his ambiguous message.

She had told Sophia about it who had been equally shocked and puzzled, shaking her head in bafflement. What did it all mean? Although she had been having a weird feeling herself, a premonition she did not want to alarm her friend so she had not said anything that something bad was going to happen, she could sense it.

* * *

CHAPTER 7

HOMECOMING

As of now she had to change the despondent mood that had fallen over her family, like a dark ominous cloud, she threw herself into full mum mode and decided to cheer her children up, especially the older one who was sad, and had withdrawn into himself. He was clearly worried, but Andromeda knowing her son all too well, also knew that he shut down and became silent. Maybe it was a form of self-preservation, but she had to coax him out of his shell if only to comfort and reassure him.

She had to stay focused, and not get entangled in her own perilous thoughts. With a defiant shrug, as if to cast off an invisible cloak of negativity that had threatened to shroud her, she busied herself in the children's preparations for their father's arrival.

They had spent the day making cards and little gifts to give to him which they were sure would delight him. Tidying away their toys and books and clothes littering the floor, it had looked like a toy store had caved in on itself, with the detritus of pencils, and colouring books and wax crayons strewn all over a huge area. This was always the best time to clean and catch up, as her children slept, exhausted by their energetic antics and running around all day.

In two days, they would be a complete family again and busy themselves. Life would return to normal. There were a lot of places her husband had promised he would take her to visit. They had made numerous plans for the future she could not wait. They had shopped to the point of excess. Their allocated garage was filled to overflowing with boxes and containers of household items they had spent weekends and long hours picking out from their scouting trips in Beijing They had bought large items from furniture to exquisite decorations Everything had been handpicked and lovingly packed for the home they were going to have built in Islamabad with scenic mountain views and lush valleys. She shuddered in delight at the prospect. Her husband was due a promotion, once they returned. They would have a lovely home to display their vast collection of purchases, from hand hewn carvings of jade and rosewood furniture and much more. Visitors to the house would be awed and fascinated with their home. She could not wait.

* * *

CHAPTER 8

THE PREMONITION

The walls were shaking and trembling with such might, as if any moment the whole structure was going to collapse, burying her beneath, before she could make a run for it. Chipped stone, and painted boards, splintered with a defiant snap breaking free from their concrete restraints. Blinding plaster dust and debris begin to trickle through the ceiling and start falling in sheets until she struggled to see anything. There was a deafening roar coming from within and around her. Andromeda stood rooted to the floor that was now vibrating and sending shock impulses through her. She could not move, immobilised by fear, as the building was imploding all around her. Dust swirled about her, as acrid fumes choked her, why was she not moving? Her body refused to budge as it stood rooted to its stop.

The door which was now rattling in its hinges beckoned her escape. She was staring right to it, but her feet refused to move. She seemed frozen to the spot. More wood splintered and the roaring grew louder as the humble edifice in which she stood snapped, crackled and fell apart. She heard someone screaming at the top of their lungs telling everyone to get out, save themselves, although there were no other persons she could see but herself.
The roof had begun caving in, the whole building trembled and shook on its foundations as an earth quake like intensity took hold of whatever came within its deadly grasp, obliterating and destroying things in a mad rampage of destruction and mayhem.

Her eyes adjusted to the light filtering through the open doorway. Inside the turmoil continued unabated, yet she could see the calm and tranquil neighbourhood beyond the open entrance unaffected by the devastation that was whipping up a frenzied storm all around her .Not a leaf stirred nor did any sound come forth as she stared past the door, an eerie calm beyond beckoned to her. It seemed unnatural She was standing between two different worlds one in which she was enveloped in the unfolding destruction paralysed to her spot outside her home all was blissfully serene and peaceful The two worlds could not have been any more different.

Was she having some out of body experience? Or was she dreaming within a dream unable to get out and break free. She was trapped in her own nightmare as the collapsing house joined the raucous of deafening sounds. The grinding and roaring of earth shattering noises seemed to be growing louder and coming closer Transfixed she could only watch in horror frozen in place as her world seemed to be collapsing around her. She was screaming to no-one in particular yet begging everyone to get out, "Save yourselves," she heard the sound of her own voice yelling. No body responded to her cries. She was all alone in her apparent anguish. There did not appear to be another living breathing soul except for herself. Where was everybody?

She wanted to move but found she could not She was paralysed and transfixed in the middle of a room, she now barely recognised as the walls had been ripped and torn down bearing the skeletal frame of ripped plaster woads and exposed brick a thunderous roar rang out. It seemed like the earth was imploding on itself. Was this how the end of the world looked like Through the gaping doorway in which the door hung limply like a disfigured tree she saw two huge monstrous earth diggers, facing her. They stood on the rim of a giant crater freshly dug out right in the centre of her garden. This was insane she clamoured to reach them but could not move.

Huge mounds of soil and clay were piled up around the edges, freshly scooped out by huge iron arms that protruded like alien beings with menacing claws of steel. The hole must have been 10 feet deep, like a sinister invitation awaiting to bury its incoming occupant.

She jolted upright drenched in perspiration and gasping for air, the sheets were suffused with sweat, heart beating wildly as if any moment it would burst from her chest. Perspiration beaded her forehead. She fought to control her breath and calm her anxiety It had been a vivid nightmare she now recalled reaching for the pitcher of water and glass next to her bedside as she poured herself a drink with trembling hands Her throat felt dry and her tongue coarse She was not feeling well at all The nightmare had spooked her and the fact that she could recall every vivid detail did little to soothe her mounting uneasiness. What was the universe trying to tell her? She wondered fear overriding all her senses.

Unbeknown to her that had been the second premonition of events building up, following the cryptic message on the computer earlier that day.

She decided to invite her friend who lived in the flat below to come and sit with her as she wasn't feeling so well after the nightmare from the previous night. They had talked well into the early hours, long after their children were tucked up in their beds and it was just after midnight

Finally, she fell into deep sleep. She sat up an hour later, pulse racing, heart in her mouth, she was perspiring and her body trembled with fear. She had just had the most awful, vivid nightmare that had shaken her to her very core. What was worse it had seemed so very real.

The accompanying feelings left her paralysed with a sense of an impending doom moving like a nocturnal beast of the night, swathed in a black cloak as dark as the darkest night, she could almost sense the claws of this unmasked predator drawing close. She could almost feel the imperceptible wrath of doom emanating from its faceless formless presence. It moved with purpose gliding towards her, a premonition of something dark and foreboding that was about to befall her entire family.

The next day the women set out for what would be just another ordinary shopping day like any other and countless others. Andromeda had decided to join her two friends and do some retail therapy. Her husband would be landing this evening after a 10-hour flight Beijing Time 18.30. He would be leaving the house in about 2 hours. It was still very early in the UK. She wondered if he had gotten any sleep at all following the late night call. He would be exhausted without question.

He had an upcoming promotion once he got back. It had been in the offing for a while now. He had worked exceptionally hard, above and beyond, for the long-awaited promotion. Andromeda knew that it would be a significant milestone in her husband's career. He had worked tirelessly to get to this place, and was considered amongst the best officers in his batch. Andromeda's heart swelled with pride, her husband deserved the promotion.

She was also aware that, such an elevation in her husband's rank meant she would also gain seniority among the military wives. She could now enjoy the coveted status of senior wife in the chain of command.

Andromeda had only ever know military life since marriage. It was a different way of life to the civil sector. A strict regime of discipline, impeccable training and world class values were embodied in the attributes of the men and their families. Living in this environment and cocooned by the high standards set by the force had, meant that Andromeda had enjoyed a life of relative luxury, ease and contentment. She found that an army officer's wife also brought great respect and reverence from everybody who knew them. This humbled her greatly to learn that in comparison to the ordinary citizen, they were considered to be elite and treated as such.

In all of the military forces combined, hierarchy was everything. Commissioned and non-commissioned officers were accorded status. Depending upon the rank, this brought with it many special privileges and benefits.

The economic concessions were a huge blessing for many families like hers. Andromeda discovered, school fees, were subsidised as were bills and staples required for running a household. They were not required to pay the same as those of the civilians residing outside the bases. The areas that she had lived in over the years were known as cantonments, they were in effect protected enclaves and Andromeda had never felt so secure, that was until now.

There would be endless parties and people coming to congratulate them, as was the custom. She wanted to be prepared for the lavish dinners and lunches she would be expected to prepare for her husband's guests. It would be a great opportunity to showcase her culinary skills and hostessing skills She had learnt a lot from her friends and the numerous parties and functions she had attended with her husband He would be so proud of her she thought excitement and joy filled her with the excited anticipation of his return.

Angelie was the wife of a biologist and one of Andromeda's closest friends. She had accompanied them today on their shopping jaunt. A tall elegant woman, who was much older in years to Andromeda and Sophie, but she maintained herself well with such grace and poise that made many a young woman envious. Having a husband in a top official ranking role and an unlimited spending budget for her to spend also helped. Despite having a considerable advantage over her friends and peers, Angelie was one of the most down to earth, humble and sincere people she had ever come known. As well as being loyal to a fault, Andromeda knew that she was blessed to have such a friend in her life. A friend who bore no airs and graces, or the superficial mannerisms of many of the diplomatic circles she had frequented. What you saw was what you got with Angelie, a wholesome, caring, and kind woman at heart.

She was like a mother to Andromeda, protective and very caring. Angelie had been living in China for many years where her husband Francis was a renowned Biologist with his own lab and a dedicated team of scientists under him who were knee deep in revolutionary research from discovering ancient marine samples to nuclear research. Their 3 children were grown up and in college, except for the youngest son, he was Samuel's age and both had become best friends in the last 3 years. Angelie knew her way around the malls, shops, and backstreets of China's buzzing commerce sector. They were regular shopping partners and had scouted half the city's main shopping thoroughfares searching for new and interesting products.

As always they had a blast. Angelie was a mischievous child at heart and brought so much joy and laughter wherever they went. Trying to contain their uncontrollable giggles they chattered animatedly walking and stopping occasionally to admire the stares and curious items on display, attracting the attention and curious glances of the natives

Andromeda had never felt as joyous and free as a bird as the time she spent in her friend's scintillating company. Though she was quite senior compared to her other two friends, Angelie was young at heart and had a refreshing young spirit that lured others to her Andromeda loved her friend very much and often sought her wisdom and counsel on many occasions.

She could not recall when she had ever laughed so much when back home in Pakistan amongst her in laws, gloomy thoughts filtered through her mind as she recalled how sad and unhappy she had felt for years until now .

They had but a few weeks left before they were returning back there as her husband's post had now ended. Quickly dispelling all thoughts aside, she decided to focus on the moment at hand determined to take whatever pockets of happiness came her way.

The future would take care of itself, she told herself self-assuredly She was not the same woman as she had been 4 years ago, that young unsure woman lacking self-confidence and a backbone had now been replaced by a more self-assured confident lady refined by the world of diplomacy and etiquette She had played hostess to delegations from over 194 countries and attended sumptuous banquets and glittering receptions dined with presidents and army chiefs of the hosting nation.

She had stood shoulder to shoulder in welcoming lines to greet heads of state Men and women she had never dreamed of meeting face to face much less shaking hands with and speaking with Andromeda had rubbed shoulders with high ranking officials and attended plush coffee mornings with wives of notable dignitaries from all over the world.

It had been an eye opening experience, Not only to see how the other half lived but to actually live like that for the entire duration she had lived there. Nothing in her view could ever top that It had been an experience of a lifetime accorded only to the very rarest of lucky individuals. She had developed close ties and forged lasting friendships with many of the ladies in the diplomatic corps. They were an amazing bunch of women who she knew would become a great part of her life. What more could a girl ask for!

There had not been a single day apart from weekends when she had not dressed up in her fine attire and jewellery to attend a function or event for there was always something going on in the days of the week She felt like Cinderella going to the ball every single day She never tired of it There would be lots of stories and anecdotes to tell her children and grandchildren one day she smiled at the thought.

Maybe once she was back home she would be the envy of her in- laws and relatives and they would even begin to notice her and the positive changes that had taken place in her from all the experiences she had had. She dared hope that they might even accord her some respect and begin to embrace her within their fold. For too long she had been a lowly black sheep cast out from the flock, now they would let her back into their fold and let bygones be bygones. She felt optimistic as her spirits leapt for joy at the thought. All she had ever wanted or could ask for was to belong in her husband's family and at the same time make him immensely proud of her as a person.

What was she going to cook today when she got home It would be her husband's favourite dish He loved biryani an exotic dish of rice and chicken blended with spices He loved her cooking despite a few unsuccessful attempts at new dishes he had never complained and ate whatever she made She smiled at the thought She would wear something nice when he came home These had been the thoughts flitting through her head as she and her friends readied themselves for the journey back home.

Chattering away and laughing they discussed their shopping, the friends gathered their purchases and made for the elevator in the shopping precinct which at the time was quite empty. It was quite early as business owners and vendors began trickling into the 4 storey mall. The noisy grinding of steel shutters could be heard from a distance as they opened up to the rumbling and the clanking of chains Alarm systems were deactivated and the noisy vendors began readying themselves for a day of busy commerce.

The three women had wanted to avoid the rush hour traffic and get the necessary shopping done, in order to be back home in time before noon.

There were not so many shoppers at this time, or perhaps because it was mainly the haunts of the diplomats and more well-heeled customers who frequented Duty free to indulge in some retail therapy on offer. The array of goods on display catering to expatriates like herself reflected expatriate prices also.

They were extortionate and inflated to a great degree, yet many of the clientele who came here didn't seem to mind. They had deep pockets and could afford to spend extravagantly with abandon. Finally she found what she had been looking for all along and, heartily made the purchase with much delight and to the amusement of her two friends. It was an exquisite set of 3 sterling silver Queen Anne serving dishes complete with candle burners to keep food warm. She beamed with a satisfactory joy filling her insides. The purchase would be her chance to showcase her hostessing and culinary skills when they invited people over. Her food and her newly acquired skills as a diplomat's wife would endear her to all and she would in turn get many invites with her husband to their homes. In the 4 years they had been here she had grown and developed a self confidence that had surprised even her. She had flourished amongst many of the families and forged great bonds with Andromeda knew that she would never forget her time here It had been a glorious time of fantastic memories she would take away with her and cherish till the end of her days.

* * *

CHAPTER 9

DUTY FREE QUEEN ANNE SILVER

Andromeda loved with abandon the hustle and bustle of the antique markets and down town bazaars lining the narrow streets that stretched for miles. Many of the places she had frequented with her husband had been a spectacular adventure in themselves.

The famous was the Panjiayuan Antique market also known as the dirt market. It was a very famous treasure trove of arts, crafts and antiques, items beyond the wildest imaginations of man.

Sunday could not arrive quickly enough for Andromeda, when her husband would take her for their weekly visit.

They never came back empty handed, although where she was going to store the burgeoning collection of antiques in her home was a problem for another day. There were only so many vases and glass ornaments and calligraphy paintings that one could put in a home, but that did not deter the retail happy women as they chattered and laughed amiably.

Today they were frequenting a different part of the city. Inside the network of markets that stretched out haphazardly, endless labyrinths twisted and turned, at odd angles, the deeper the further they went. It was hard not to stop and gawk at the spectacular array of goods on display at each stall and market place. Andromeda stared at the strange and weird objects in fascination. She loved it. Everything about China so far that she had seen was an immense cultural eye-opening experience. So far removed from her British and Pakistani way of life.

This was China after all, little groups of men, possibly labourers and farmers relaxing over a game of Mahjong and sipping green tea, with the occasional erupting of their raucous laughter and protests as all the dice clattered noisily on the boards.

The friends were chatting animatedly as they lazily mounted the escalator and let its slow rhythmic momentum carry them out onto the top of the first level where they gingerly stepped off and proceeded on their way through the expansive double glass doorway which led out into the busy street which branched out into many densely packed stall lined passages on each side of the main road It was a cacophony of colour noise and sights as shoppers mingled with vendors at every corner.

The narrow passages were little more than side streets winding and alluring to Andromeda. Everywhere she looked she was dazzled by the exotic items on display This beat her usual shopping trips to Asda or Tescos back home. She had never seen such an array of curiosities and exotic handcrafted treasures as those that were on display. Everything to her delight and astonishment was spectacular Even the food markets held a vast array of consumable items she could not even name

It was a vision to behold the Chinese people were renowned for eating one of the healthiest diets in the world They always ate fresh huge quantities of vegetables and grass fed meats, as well as a large variety of seafood with herbs and spices that Andromeda had never heard of Their diet was lean and rich in nutrients From hotpots to dumplings and stir fried delicacies

Andromeda had sampled some the countries famous cuisine but she was far from developing an acquired palate for many of the things that had been served to her in the many Chinese banquets and dinners she had attended .One look at the beautifully presented concoctions on her plate or soup bowls containing the odd sharks fin had only lessened her appetite just as the highly preferred delicacies of stinky tofu hens claws, oxtail even snake meat had found its way on her plate and it had been all she could do to stop herself from throwing up Her husband and children on the other hand were far more adventurous compared to her and sampled everything. She obviously had a less of an acquired palate than her family.

On many occasions Andromeda would return home from an event hungry and ravenous only to end up getting a McDonalds from one of the many American Franchises that were liberally scattered about in the bustling heart of Beijing.

Today it had started out like any other ordinary shopping day with her friends except it was to turn out to be one of the darkest periods of her life emblazoned forever into her memory. A day she never thought she would live to see.

Traffic bustled past, with the incessant blares of horns and indignant drivers gesticulating wildly at no one in particular, the noise of vendors shouting, competing over one another at the passing throngs of people. Voices mingled with the roar of motor vehicles, and buzz of life permeated the air. It was getting busier. The midday sun was starting to cast its sweltering rays as the people moved imperviously beneath, some ducking beneath awnings or seeking the shade of trees lining the dusty roads.

Suddenly Andromeda felt the buzzing of her mobile, it was vibrating with relentless persistence. Her hands were full as she scrambled to locate it in her pockets, clutching haphazardly to her array of bags and packages to prevent them from tumbling onto the cracked pavement.

The 3 friends had enjoyed quite a shopping spree and were all armed with bags, ready for the journey home. Andromeda finally managed to grab her mobile and put it to her ear, supporting it with her chin as she tilted her head to listen, whilst trying to maintain a grip on her parcels. She listened attentively, the colour slowly draining from her face, as a deathly pallor appeared. The sound of wind rushing and a roaring began to build up in her ear as she felt herself tumble into nothingness.

* * *

CHAPTER 10

HE IS DEAD

From the moment that call blared out its vibrant Ed Sheeran beat, Andromeda remembered nothing else. Her parcels, slipped from her now clammy hands as she lost her grasp, her unseeing eyes barely registering as they clattered noiselessly onto the chipped pavement. She felt herself stumble as she let out an anguished wail, and collapsed on the broken pavement, narrowly avoiding a cyclist pulling a cart filled with vegetables. He swerved violently to avoid the stricken women, overturning a couple of baskets, as the cart dangerously tilted spilling its contents. Cabbages, aubergines, and tomatoes were sent tumbling down the road, onto the broken footpath, squashed, and squelched by passing feet.

Furious and enraged, the angry, Chinese man, whose face had turned scarlet with fury, let loose a tirade of unintelligible Mandarin, shaking his fists at the women as people stopped to stare. A few passers-by had stopped to retrieve the vegetables that had survived impact , pocketing a few when they thought no-one was looking and helped the old man who was spouting angry mandarin on the confused looking trio of women standing a few yards from the upturned cart . Clearly the women were foreigners and seemed totally distracted from the chaos they had just caused, they seemed to be in the midst of their own private turmoil as they held up a young girl who looked to be on the verge of collapse, her young face creased in some inexplicable grief, clearly contorted with pain. By now a considerable throng had gathered to watch the spectacle. If the angry shouts and cries of the vendor had not alerted them, the women standing to one side of the overturned cart supporting one of their own, had got their attention.

What was going on here, they wondered? By now they were used to the countless barrage of tourists and foreigners swarming like flies, traipsing in their hordes through the never-ending maze of markets and precincts. China had so much to offer and the variety of wares they produced made it a central hub of commercial activity worldwide. The exotic displays of merchandise attracted customers from very region of the globe, so it was little surprise to see foreigners hunting for treasures and filling the markets with their presence. They were everywhere.

The vendor who had turned several shades of crimson by now , having righted his cart with the help of some young men was still in the midst of his tirade , was shaking his meaty fist profusely towards the women ,as he ventured forth , taking a determined step forward , so that he could confront the foreigners , something made him stop in his tracks ,as he stared straight ahead , he then registered the crumpled form of the young woman, clutching the arm of her friend as another lady tried to lift her off the floor where she had collapsed in a heap . They were trying to console an inconsolable Andromeda by now, who was sobbing hysterically amidst a growing crowd of curious onlookers.

Her horrified friends, in that instant had rushed to grab hold of her elbow on each side and catch her in their arms. They tried in vain to make sense of what she was. By this time, Andromeda was babbling incoherently. Through her raucous sobs and anguished tears, her friends could not get any sense out of her. "What on earth had happened?" they wondered in shocked puzzlement.

One of her friends grabbed Andromeda's phone from her shaking hands and spoke to whoever it was on the line, and after listening intently for a few minutes, her face too, took on a pale white hue, as if she had spoken to a ghost. Crumpled in disbelief and shock, she turned to the other friend and told her what had happened, as tears began to cascade freely down her cheeks.

They had learnt that Andromeda's husband had died in the early hours this morning. After talking to his wife, he had suffered a major cardiac episode from which he did not recover and now preparations were in earnest to bring his remains back to be buried in his ancestral village.

As onlookers gathered, and the Chinese watched on in morbid fascination, uncomprehending and almost enjoying the plight of these three women of one who was clearly distressed and in a terrible state. Her friends grappled to get Andromeda on her feet. Unsteady and ashen faced with shock, she was trembling as if her inner core had been suffused with nitrogen, her blood was running cold and her heart was slowing down dangerously.

They managed to hail a passing taxi and had made it clumsily through the growing throng of more gathered people and carts as they followed the two sobbing women who were trying to hold up the third one in a bystander effect.

No one moved as people just froze on the sidewalk, mouths agape, some gesticulating towards the trio as they talked with their companions, with mild but curious amusement. In their hectic labour driven lives, where work and home was all they knew amidst the daily rigours of trying to earn a crust, it was not every day that one got to see live drama unfold in front of them.

One of Andromeda's friends managed to flag down a yellow taxi, urgently beckoning to it to come closer, as one hand held firm to Andromeda's slumped back. The car rolled up, and stopped near the kerb, as more people, and curious onlookers who had drawn closer to watch the unfolding spectacle stepped back a few paces to give the women room.

The women struggled but managed to lift their perplexed and confused friend into the back seat, ensuring she was placed in the middle so that they sat on either side to support their distraught friend. Their own silent tears mingled with sympathy and unbearable pity for their young friend's loss.

She was only 30 and now a young widow in the blink of an eye. Her 4 young children were now fatherless. It was heart wrenching, and so surreal. Andromeda slumped, and sobbing, leant against her friends, repeating the words in a whisper, almost, 'He's dead. He's dead, he's left me, he can't be, tell me it's not true.' The two women struggled to contain their emotions as they glanced over Andromeda's bowed head at each other, eyes brimming with tears and unspeakable sadness. Their own hearts were breaking to watch their young friend's whole life implode. It was all they could do but hold her, comfort her and wipe her torrent of tears while trying to contain their own, which now flowed freely.

The driver, an elderly Chinese in his sixties, moved off slowly, and expertly negotiating his way through the now busy thoroughfare of people, carts and bikes and everything else that fought to occupy the narrow pavements and pot holed roads, they eventually joined the main bypass road that would take them all the way to their district. It was a 40-minute drive, but everything passed by in a blur, it was hard to tell.

Time had stood still since the onset of the news, yet everything seemed to be racing past at breakneck speed as if she had lost control over her ability to be in the present.

* * *

CHAPTER 11

GET THEM OUT

It was a warm day, the atmosphere in the taxi was stifling as the two women, one on either side of Andromeda, holding her arm to support her, looked pale and shocked to the core struggling to keep their own emotions under check.

One of her friends adjusted her position to pull the window down to let in some fresh air, in the hope that it would revive the stricken Andromeda, whose colour had taken on a deathly pallor when she had taken the first call. She looked like she was going to pass out any second, the colour of her skin had taken on an unnatural deathly pallor. Her lips were dry and cracked, they had tried to give her some water but she had refused, too numb to take anything.

The silence in the taxi was broken by choked sobs and sniffling, as the two friends tried to soothe and console a devastated Andromeda who was slumped over and struggling between gasps to comprehend what was happening to her. It was as if someone had ruthlessly snatched the rug from under her feet, her whole life had turned on its axle. She was spinning into a black gaping hole of nothingness.

It was surreal, she thought, through intermittent clouds of clarity, this could not be happening to her. It was the stuff that one read about and only happened to others. She felt dizzy and her mouth dry, as her head pounded with such velocity, it felt like her brains would explode and shatter just like her broken heart which lay in hundreds of tiny shards.

Eventually the taxi drew to a halt in front of Andromeda's flat.

As they gently helped her out, after paying the fare, they led the distraught Andromeda towards the building. She was still repeating and reliving the conversation she had had on the phone with her son a few moments earlier. What did they mean? He was sick and they were bringing him back to Pakistan for treatment? Why were they telling her the news in a perceptible state of distress with the sound of loud, anguished sobs, and crying in the background. It did not make any sense.

She could still hear the distinct noises of crying and the unmistakeable wails emanating through the phone. Her younger brother whom she had not seen in years or spoken to, was the one who had delivered the stricken news to her eldest son, who was in a state of shock and had called Andromeda to tell her to come home straight away.

Why had they told her over the phone that her husband had taken ill and was on his way home to Pakistan for treatment? Why on earth would they take him there? Bypassing some of the best medical facilities in the world and specialist treatments, available in the UK to be treated instead in his homeland where resources were few, scant and expensive at best and those who could afford better treatment often travelled abroad than risk complications at the hands of inadequately equipped surgeons. It made no sense whatsoever to Andromeda.

What on earth had happened to him to be taken so ill? Hundreds of questions sped through her mind. With the chilling dread of realisation that she tried to eradicate, knowing in her gut that the worst had happened, her husband was dead.

As the taxi turned into their compound slowing down her thoughts drifted to the phone call. Her son's heart wrenching voice as he tried to summon the terrifying words in between his choking sobs, telling his mother to come home immediately His voice displayed a panic she had never heard before. A call from the UK, a few moments earlier from Andromeda's brother had clearly unsettled him.

She could barely understand a word as he was crying too much. She needed to get home this very instant. It was at that moment Angelie had taken the phone from her friend's shaking hands and listened briefly before hanging up. Almost immediately her husband had rang her mobile to confirm their worst fears, that Andromeda's husband had suffered a fatal cardiac event and the people at the embassy had been notified as had the family members back in Pakistan.

It had been a harrowing call as no one could quite believe it, he had been a young officer with so much promise and his star had been on the rise, now people were stunned in disbelief at the shocking news outbreak. They could not quite get their heads around it. It had caught everyone unawares, least of all his own family, 4 children now left without a father, wife without her husband, a mother without her son.

Preparations were being made to repatriate his remains back to his native village.

As Andromeda clamoured and clawed her way through a misty haze of confused and numbing thoughts, and the one very brief conversation she had had with her son, she knew already in that heart stopping instance. They did not have to spell it out for her. This was what all the signs of the last few days had been leading up to all along. This was what her dreams and nightmares had been preparing her for the ambiguous message sent by her husband the late night call of concern, and a host of other subtle signs.

Though nobody had said it outright and were trying to deliver the awful news as gently as possible, she knew with heavy certainty in her heart, that she was now a widow, and her children now orphaned.

* * *

CHAPTER 12

MOURNERS GATHERING

The door was flung wide open, which was unusual as her children were under strict orders to keep it locked at all times when she was not home. You just never knew, there were intruders, and burglars everywhere looking to seize upon an opportunity to ransack a place. You could never be too safe.

As they led her inside, she stopped in her tracks as she looked with comprehending horror and understanding at the many people from her husband's work place gathered here in her home.

What more was terrifying, in those brief moments, was the confirmation written in everybody's faces, of the news, Andromeda hoped and prayed would not be true. Her husband of 16 years was dead.

They looked at her despondently, stricken with tears and palpable grief as more people crowded into their humble flat. No one daring to speak, just sobbing quietly into their handkerchiefs. She could feel dozens of pairs of eyes on her now gaunt looking face.

They all stared but did not move or speak. Occasional gasps of horror followed by soft words of sympathy as they looked her way and just as swiftly averted their eyes. People shook their heads in utter disbelief, looking at one another but at Andromeda, No one could find the courage to make eye contact with Andromeda. Her loss was immeasurable, there were no words to comfort the young woman.

Nothing anyone could say could ease the pain and trauma, she was experiencing at this very moment. A look of total incomprehension and shock etched Andromeda's tear stained face, as Angelie held her close, stroking her hair and wiping her tears at the same time as controlling her own. She was the closest to family that Andromeda had right now. Angelie would stay by her side as her husband made all the necessary arrangements.

In the ensuing days, preparations to fly her family out to Pakistan were made, a condolence ceremony was arranged at the embassy for the people who thronged in their hundreds to come and pay their respects and make their final farewells.

Her husband had been a popular man, and everyone who had known him and met him, had been swayed by his magnetic charms and effusive personality. There had been very few who had not been pulled in by his wickedly roguish charms and endearing nature. She could not believe that she was thinking of her husband in the past tense. These kind of things only happened to other people. This was not happening to her.

The room was filled with the urgent whispers and the shuffling of feet as people entered the room and some moved aside to make way for new comers, the atmosphere was as morbid as the occasion befitted. Andromeda hung limply against Angelie. Every few seconds she would prop herself up, and with a wide eyed stare, she looked around wildly at the mass of people gathered in her flat. She bore the look of a mad woman as she demanded in a voice hoarse with crying, for everyone to leave.

Why were they staring at her like that? Why did no one venture to speak? Had she grown a set of horns, these people she and her husband had wined and dined with now stood immobilised like strangers scrutinising her intently. Sadness and the apparent pitying expressions, masked their faces. They watched beneath close hooded eyes, moist with tears at the young woman bereft in her grief folded into a hunched form as Angelie held her close sitting down beside her on the sofa as everyone gathered silently around her The flat was very cramped and too small, for the number of people that now stood and watched in silent disbelieving horror

Why were they just staring at her like she was some alien entity whom they're seeing for the first time? A hush had descended upon the small flat interspersed with sniffling and silent sobs and the rustle of handkerchiefs as noses were blown and sighs could be heard amongst gentle whispers.

It was strange how so many people, with more arriving by the second could fit into her cramped flat.

Her mind drifted to the mundane and ordinary practicalities despite her state of unbelieving shock. After a short while Angelie had led Andromeda who had sat slumped and listless on the uncomfortable settee to the bedroom where her friend placed some cushions and adjusted a pillow behind her barely conscious friend and with the assistance of another woman whose husband worked in the commercial sector and they were also close friends helped to prop up limp form of their friend as she dropped back against the bed board for support

Her eyes swollen and bloodshot with grief and tears that were yet to bring forth a bigger deluge of grief as reality slowly began to seep in. There was no way he could be dead, her mind was telling her it was a cruel prank She had only spoken to him no less than 12 hours ago. Then why did all these steadily arriving people appear otherwise. Their mournful faces belied anything other than her worst fear. Her husband was not coming back ever!

It was then after what seemed like a long stretched out silence that her eyes shifted to her left where the 3 door wardrobe stood with its door half open Through the gaping cupboard door a clothes rail packed tightly with an array of clothes. His clothes and jackets along with all his other stuff all crammed together in the limited space. Gazing in a surreal glance she stared at the neatly lined array of shoes and brogues her husband had amassed all waiting for him to walk in any second and pick out a pair to wear.

They had often joked that it was normally the woman who was renowned for taking up more closet space and not having enough shoes. Her husband had more matching outfits than she had and they often laughed about it
She felt embarrassed and mortified about the messy state of her flat. Everything looked so dishevelled and out of place.

What would these people think, of her slovenly, disorganised home? She had not been expecting any visitors or she would have tidied up and made it more presentable. Why on earth would her mind not reign it in, she was losing it, thinking about a tidy flat when her entire world had just imploded. Her thoughts were in disarray as she tried to grapple with the swirling confusion in her head.

* * *

CHAPTER 13

SURREAL

Why are these people here in our flat? Where are my kids? I feel terrible, but I am confused, is this really happening to me?

The horrors had been finally brought to bare in their gruesome reality. All those bone, mind numbing feelings she had been experiencing had turned into her very own living nightmare. Her senses had frozen taken her far back to the time when she had first met her husband, all the events in between, the struggle to keep their marriage afloat. Her brain refused to make sense of what her heart already knew to be true. It all came rushing back, that sinking feeling as she had lain in her bed the night before, knowing deep down that her husband was gone.

That sense of foreboding, the awareness of heightened senses were all telling her that something bad was going to happen. Dark clouds were making their way across the stillness of her thoughts, slowly curling their gnarled hands across her mind casting it in a shadow which plunged any rational thought or reason into a place where darkness was beckoning to her. It was inviting her to join it and to be enveloped into its forbidding depths.

The dream, the call in the night, his last words to her. The declaration of love as he left for the airport as she left for her teaching at the Montessori school. He even promised her that upon his return he would take them all on a trip around Europe. Words that would later prove to be prophetic.

He had been a good father to their children. The marriage had not been a cake walk but they had made the best of it for the sake of the children, despite the enormous strain they were under themselves due to many outlying factors. Living in close proximity with her in laws under one roof especially where there was ever present tension and conflict in the house made it all the more difficult to cope It was hardly surprising Andromeda found that this only led to further arguments between her husband and herself Whenever they did manage to find themselves alone which was rare except at night times he did not want to know. Even in their private moments Andromeda was frustrated to observe her husband shutting down refusing to hear anything about her struggles and the day's events, anything that bordered upon his family it was a closed chapter as far as he was concerned.

There seemed to be no solution at hand Andromeda thought in resigned defeat. Her husband was adamant that he was doing the right thing supporting his family by keeping them with him. He was oblivious to his wife's unhappiness and unperturbed by the conflicts that flared up around his wife on a daily basis.

As far as he was concerned she had to figure it out and make peace with his family no matter what they did or said It was her problem and she had to deal with it as his wife which meant utter subservience and respect towards his family There were no compromises and budging from his stance He simply chose to turn a deaf ear at his wife's protests of being overworked and underappreciated She was being ungrateful and acting like a spoilt child in his view.

There had been no point she told herself sullenly. The discord and bitterness continued to fester like a slow moving disease.

In spite of everything that had happened Andromeda had been a dependant wife looking to her husband for everything He provided for her and the children now she was going to have to do that all by herself and she had no idea how

How had it come to this Her husband gone before his time, without any warning he had not been ill as far as she was aware A sudden inexplicable death No one could fathom how it had happened so suddenly catching everyone off guard It had turned their lives upside down, leaving Andromeda all alone with 4 children to take care of.

He was going to miss every milestone of their lives, the graduations, the marriages, the births of their children. They in turn were going to grow up without that one solid presence of a father to hold their hands and guide them through the rocky treacherous slopes of life. The help and support, the love unconditional, the guidance he would have given her and the children in their developmental years.

* * *

CHAPTER 14

DENIAL

The moment she had received the news, waves of shock and numbness had begun to seep in. She fought the urge to believe what had just happened yet somehow, she could feel herself being picked up and propelled at great speed into the eye of one raging and ferocious storm.

Shock waves resonated within her as she grappled with this tsunami of grief which was enveloping her all the while. She mustn't lose it, she could not succumb to uncontrollable despair, especially now, there were her children to think of, yes, her fatherless, now orphaned children. She would not let herself be consumed by the weight of her grief that was pressing down upon her on all sides, until she felt that every particle of her being would shatter into a million pieces. She had to hold it together.

Somewhere, amongst the layers of emotions and paralysing grief that were invading her body, as she tried to grasp the magnitude, and the horrendous implications of being widowed, left alone to raise 4 children by herself, it was the thought of her children that pulled her back from the looming precipice. A strength somewhere in the deep recesses of her soul was surfacing, she had to fight this, and get a grip on herself, and her composure and iron will was needed to help her distraught children.

They were young, very confused, and heartbroken, their lives lay in tatters unless she took control. Her youngest child barely 2 years old could not comprehend what had happened. It broke her heart to see their small tear stained faces. Too young to even understand, much less grasp the enormity of their loss. Amidst her racing thoughts, Andromeda barely noticed the overwhelming throngs of people who had silently begun to gather in her small flat to pay their respects.

* * *

CHAPTER 15

CONDOLENCE

The book of condolences was set up in the embassy where her husband had been stationed with his family. As phones began to ring incessantly, mobiles going off in all directions, hurried voices and urgent whispers could be heard all around her. She was oblivious to it all but aware at the same time.

Andromeda could see the unbidden silent tears flowing and stifled sobs as downcast expressions on everyone's faces only reiterated her sorry plight.

Someone somewhere was taking care of her children in the other room. It was only a tiny flat yet Andromeda wondered how it was possible to fit so many people in such a cloistered space.

She almost felt the urge to let out a giggle, likening her flat to the Tardis from the infamous Dr Who series, her shock was beginning to manifest as her thoughts wandered erratically in a haphazard display of confusion. More and more people who knew and worked with her husband had started arriving and gathering in their small apartment when the news had broken.

It was all very surreal. Surely this was not happening, she was dreaming, just a nightmare from which she would wake up any moment except it was real, and this was her worst nightmare come true.

Her head was pounding, about to explode and her eyes burnt as the tears were unstoppable. At times she felt herself being held and consoled and the voices gradually started to grow fainter, she was shutting out the noise and her eyes felt heavy. Maybe she had dozed for a few minutes as she jolted upright to sit up in the bed where she had lain.

Some people had left and some were there issuing directives to start the process of extraction for Andromeda and the children to fly out back to Pakistan where she would be escorted straight to the village for the funeral.

It sounded incongruously strange to her own ears those forbidden words in the same sentence, husband, funeral, death, Widow Everything felt like a blur surreal, as if it was happening to someone else and she was just a bystander Then why did she feel so numb her limbs felt paralysed and her mouth dry, why was everyone looking at her with such stark pity in their eyes.

* * *

CHAPTER 16

HANG IN THERE

She cast a sideways glance at the fitted wardrobe in their bedroom, one of the sliding mirrored doors was open laying bare all his clothes and an assortment of coloured jackets he had been so fond of, though some Andromeda had found quite unflattering, but it was matter of personal taste.

Her husband had been the proverbial clothes horse. He knew how to work a room, and attract attention.

His patent black shoes and brogues of every description cluttered the bottom of the wardrobe. It seemed like any moment he would come through the door and grab a change of clothes before heading off to some event. Instead the clothes, the shoes, even the tangy citrus and wood scent of his aftershave lingered expectantly, for its owner.

She swallowed a sob in her throat and tried not to succumb to the nauseating feeling that was threatening to overwhelm her. Her temples throbbed and her throat was hoarse from crying, she had barely slept and eaten since her last call with her husband.

Through the swift and efficient administrations of her husband's office staff and colleagues, flights were booked and Andromeda in almost a zombie like state didn't realise until she was sat on a flight with her children to return to Pakistan where her journey to her village would begin. They gave her sedatives throughout the 16-hour flight which involved a transit stop and a plane change.

She managed to draw upon some hidden reserves of strength and gather her grieving children to her. Right now, she had to put her own feelings and emotions on hold. For all their sakes she had to keep it together and help them through this life changing event

* * *

CHAPTER 17

DUST TO DUST - RETURN HOME

The village represented the dismantling of Andromeda's mental and psychological well-being. It was the place from where it had all started, and that day, December 30th the day her husband had been laid to rest .This was where her dreams, her hopes , her plans with her husband had ultimately come to a bitter end with the finality of the last curtain call.

He had been on a short visit to the UK from where he was to return a day before his death. From the moment she had received the shocking news on the phone, she was despatched with her children on a flight from China to Pakistan.

When she had disembarked from the car that had been sent to pick her and her children from the airport, she was met with the apocalyptic scenes of grief as thousands of people's moans and shrieks filled the air. Inconsolable chants and loud crying was heard for miles from the house, as more and more mourners arrived in their droves, for Andromeda's husband had been a popular and much loved figure to many.

The mourners paved the short way for Andromeda as she slowly made her way to the middle of the courtyard where a solitary bed was placed upon which her husband was laid out. Flanked by hundreds of jostling, weeping relatives and family, someone pushed them aside so that she would not have to. He looked peaceful as if he was sleeping. Though it had been almost a week getting his body readied and transported from UK, he seemed to show no signs of death.

Andromeda stood mute, and rooted to the spot as people jostled and pushed for space around her, in the already overcrowded courtyard, all vying for a glimpse of the dead body of her husband, laid out like a prize catch on display oblivious to the stricken wails and lamentations in the air.

She watched, and tried to process this as her numbed body refused to comply with her attempts to walk where he lay. No one had come forward from her in-laws' to take her in their arms and console her. They were so wrapped up in their own grief. She felt a warm hand lightly touch her shoulder and turned to see who it was.

Upon seeing her grief-stricken parents, standing there with tears streaming down their cheeks, she fell into her father's outstretched arms and embraced her parents as her convulsive sobs took hold. They had arrived a few hours ago from the UK accompanying her husband's remains. She was at least grateful for their presence amidst the cacophony of grief now surrounding her.

She felt... empty, shock; numbness had taken hold, it was her children she thought of, they needed protecting, she had to be strong and brace herself for what had happened and what was to come. This was no time to think about herself, her whole world had collapsed but she still had her children to think about. For their sakes, she had to pull herself together.

He was gone, she was here and his family were already treating her to cold barely concealed hatred and vitriol apparent for all to see etched on their worn grief-stricken faces. Andromeda remained impassive, unmoving trying to take in everything all at once. She was mute, as voices bombarded her all around. She was dimly aware of being on autopilot trying to comprehend the gravity of her situation. For even now in the maelstrom of his sudden death, she felt the friendless, hostile glances thrown her way, the sickening pity and even barely restrained glee of some of the relatives who had had an axe to grind with her for years.

Miraculously Andromeda managed in these extraordinary circumstances to maintain some semblance of composure, much to the irritation of her in-laws. What did they expect prone as they were to primordial displays of outlandish grief? From past experience she was certainly not going to start tearing strips from her clothes, and pulling out big clumps of her hair and rolling about in the dust like someone possessed. Someone in the midst of a psychotic attack. Andromeda by some divine inner strength was able to compose herself with decorum, if only for the sake of her devastated children. She had to remain strong so she could be the cushion for them to fall on amidst their heart wrenching grief.

They needed her now more than ever as of this moment. She was their only parent. She had to keep it together. The tears would come later and when they did, she feared she would drown in their deluge. Already she had felt that huge gaping void well up inside her chest, a hole her husband had now left with his death, which she knew could consume her if she let herself waver. As of this moment her children's survival depended upon her own. She could do this. She would do this come what may.

* * *

CHAPTER 18

LAID TO REST – ANCESTRAL VILLAGE

He lay there on the Charpoi, a traditional woven bed, flanked by relatives and villagers on all sides. Stone cold to the touch, he looked peaceful as if he was merely taking a nap, oblivious to the outpouring of grief around him and the tumultuous devastation about to be unfurled upon his children and wife who were both now fatherless and husbandless.

There was very little comfort to be gleaned by the mass of people milling around because not everyone was loathe to conceal their total hatred and apparent glee at Andromeda's new widowed status. A woman fallen from grace and reduced to a pitiful state. In general widows and divorcees commanded very little respect as far as some families were concerned. She was no exception, Andromeda discovered to her dismay. The only compassion to be had, came from her shocked and grief-stricken parents and a few trusted friends.

The open hostility was laid bare for all to witness as the raw emotion rippled through the late evening breeze. For years her in laws had plagued her with their continuous insults all throughout her marriage, now they did not bother to hide their disdain. Neither did they make any attempt to disguise their animosity towards her. It had not escaped the attention of the attending mourners and guests who had flocked to the village to pay their respects. Everyone felt a surge of sympathy and pain for the young widowed Andromeda and her children.

The guests had arrived in their hundreds at the village home. Tents had to be set up to accommodate the mourners, and relatives. They would not linger after the funeral rites but return back to their respective homes. Only the close relatives would stay over, who had travelled far. This included her husband's uncles and aunts and their families, which was normally the custom.

It was not long before some of the guests that included women from distinguished families when an inappropriate outburst caught everyone unawares as people stopped what they were doing to turn towards the commotion Andromeda had been sat quietly in a corner with her mother who had flown in with the remains of her husband's body from the UK. Father had been outside sat outside in the 'Batik' a room resaved for the men of the household and external male guests. They had been trying to comfort their distraught daughter and their confused weeping grandchildren when Andromeda's mother in-law unleashed vitriol laced expletives towards an already visibly shaken and fragile Andromeda.

Everyone had stopped to pause what they were doing and turned to watch the drama unfold in the courtyard Some shook their heads in disbelief others muttered words of exasperation at the blatant lack of sympathy towards Andromeda who stood with head bowed in quiet shock as her mother in law rained down a sea of profanities on her At this point one of the sister in laws who had heard the fracas had been busy issuing instructions in the kitchen before she strode over to take her mother's arm and escort her away from making a further scene .

Andromeda would not be surprised if they had engineered the wrath of their mothering the first place by filling her ears with complaints about her as was their custom.

Aware that she was drawing attention and creating a scene finally her daughters led away their shrieking screaming mother as Andromeda wept profusely in her shocked mothers arms They were blaming her for her husband's death Mother was too shocked to respond and taken aback by the vicious verbal assault towards her daughter One of the female guests laid a calm hand on mother's arm that was holding her sobbing daughter and spoke softly Ignore these people they are illiterate and consumed by anger and grief .

They are in the wrong everyone here in attendance can see that. It is despicable to treat your daughter in this way Please take Andromeda and your grandchildren far away from them back to the UK. She will be safe there and away from these animals Mother nodded her head and choked back the sob edged in her throat aware that the woman was speaking the truth

What they were unable to say out loud when her husband was alive, was raging forth like an unstoppable wave. She was and had been at the receiving end of their wrath for years, so much so that they had wanted her husband to leave her and marry again. Tragically he had died, but now they had no inhibitions about casting her out, good riddance to her and her children.

The gloves were off, there was no holding back.

Her husband was buried with full military honours that depicted the life and duty of a glorious officer, husband, son and father. He was laid to rest amidst the pomp and ceremony befitting a 5-star general with a 21-gun salute. Her husband could not have asked for a greater tribute.

Although there had been a phenomenal turnout for her husband's funeral from ranking officers to 4 star generals, even the women, her in laws had rushed to the site of the burial place to watch beneath their concealed veils the unfolding ceremony and laying her husband to rest, she had been prevented from doing so herself, thereby missing the last opportunity to bid farewell to her husband and witness the wonderful tribute that he had been given in his final journey.

It came as an unwelcome shock to her later when everyone had returned home after the burial that she discovered they had deliberately kept her at home, deciding for her that she would not venture out to the family's burial plot which was situated in the small village and accessible by foot. They had robbed her of the one and only chance to witness her husband's last journey in which hundreds of people had come to pay their respect and amongst the large throng of mourners, only her presence was missing. She would never forgive them for that.

Her son's had been there at least taken to the grave site by a compassionate relative or a friend of her husband to see their father buried with honours.

* * *

CHAPTER 19

FIRST NIGHT, LAST GOODBYE

Following the funeral, Andromeda had learnt that it an official ceremony had been conducted with full military honours, courtesy of the Navy. Many personnel and seniors had travelled to take part she had been told, Andromeda had been prevented from witnessing the scene and had dutifully complied whereas everyone flocked to the site where the burial took place.

It had angered her at the time, unknown to her, many of her husband's friends and colleagues had tried to see her to convey their condolences and express their sympathy. They had travelled a great distance to watch the fallen soldier, one of their own, be buried with the dignity and ceremony he deserved. It had created a ripple of concern among them and no less surprising to discover they had been repeatedly refused access to Andromeda, by her in laws who cited various excused that she was not up to seeing people and that she was grieving and it was best to leave her alone. They would make sure she received their messages of condolence. Messages that Andromeda would never receive.

That first evening after the burial rites had ended and her husband had now been laid to rest in his final resting place, forever at peace, people had begun to make their farewells. Most of the official guests had departed and many relatives who had travelled far and wide left amid tearful goodbye and condolences, the shock still palpable upon many faces. He had been a significant presence in all their lives, and to be here in his home village burying him defied all sound reason and logic, especially as he had been in his prime, but death does not differentiate.

Back in the house, things were getting back to normal in the instant following the funeral. Could things ever be normal again at least for her? Andromeda thought in silent anguish.

'The village women had arrived early to partake in the mourning ritual common to these remote rural areas. They sat on starched cotton sheets, used to the uncomfortably hard uneven surface beneath them of the dirt caked ground. A quiet buzzing sound hummed across the courtyard as they spoke in hushed tones, the occasional wail or lament rang out piercing the otherwise awkward stillness of the air. Andromeda's mother in law sat forlornly in their midst, nodding her head now and then to a sympathetic comment, looking anything but like her usual matriarchal self assured self. She too was a woman broken by the loss of her son

Andromeda had risen to use the bathroom. As she walked a couple steps, she felt an overwhelming sinking sensation like a huge force, cold and weighty, dragging her down into deeper depths within her. It had seemed to grasp hold of her insides like a voracious beast. She felt dizzy and a shrill ringing sensation increasing in intensity began sounding in her ear. She could barely take a few steps to the little hut that housed the toilet. Her feet refused to comply. Her body tried to do what had come effortlessly, for years, to be able to move with ease and without thought, but now it was as if the same body was freezing up and causing each action to unfold with stiff reluctance. Her whole abdomen felt like there was a huge boulder that had lodged itself inside her, causing her to move with a slowness and a decrepitude she was unfamiliar with. Could it be shock she wondered that was manifesting itself and creeping into every ounce of her being? It would not be surprising as

Thankfully, one of Andromeda's close friends, Khadijah, had been with her since she arrived with her children. The family had befriended one another during their time in China and now she was very grateful to have her comforting presence by her side.

A huge weight was bearing down upon her, blackness tinging the horizon of her senses. She felt the firm but reassuring squeeze of her friend's arm on her own, leading her gently away from the gathered throng of mourners scattered about the courtyard. Dozens of pairs of eyes followed the two friends as they made their way gingerly to the opposite side of the courtyard

Inching slowly forward one slow step at a time, Andromeda found that her whole body had frozen in shock she was struggling to move her organs it seemed had seized up and she felt like she was encapsulated in a big solid chunk of ice. It was as if her internal organs had frozen over and refused to comply. She looked at her friend with clear anguish and grief-stricken eyes, the light gone from them only to be placed with dull lifelessness. She turned to her friend and said to her, "Something is wrong, I don't feel well at all." She felt an icy tremor of cold ripple through her insides.

Her friend, concern etched on her pretty features, immediately held her friend close and after they had managed to get to the wash room facilities, she sat Andromeda back down and gave her some water to drink with a tablet to calm her.

Andromeda was now feeling the raw shock following the news outbreak, and the initial hours of trying to process everything, followed by hours of travelling and burying her husband; the toll was showing. Until now she had been on auto pilot, her senses numbed, as she had gone through the motions with cold, calculated unfeeling movements. Her body and mind had taken over in their unified quest to carry her along in her barely conscious state.

She looked up from her stricken state and felt the piercing stares from a hundred pairs of eyes it seemed, pity, sympathy, nonchalance, mild curiosity emanating from their blatant stares. Every so often the air would ring out with the mournful sounds of a villager wailing and lamenting, an outward display of grief that was commonplace in villages. It was also not uncharacteristic for these village women to expect some sort of monetary contribution.

After the burial ceremony, 40 days' mourning was declared. Although in the Quran it was stipulated that 3 was the norm and sufficient for communal grieving, Andromeda's in-laws were determined to stick to the pre-established customs of the generations past. Huge hulking cauldrons of food had been prepared the first three days, by enlisting specially hired cooks from nearby villages. It was like a morbid feast of sorts to honour the deceased.

It was drawing towards dusk and the air took on a slightly chilly tone. It was an open courtyard. She wrapped her arms around her legs to keep warm, not comprehending, not thinking, and just numb. She spotted her parents, bless them. They had flown in from the UK with her husband's remains and the grief was so palpable on their faces that she wanted to get up and hug them. They seemed to have aged considerably in a day.

Features ravaged and worn out by the magnitude of the tragedy that had befallen their daughter and her children. Their hearts had broken when they had heard the news of their daughter becoming a widow.

It was the kind of news that no parent ever wants to experience with their child. It had destroyed her parents in a single moment All the hopes and dreams and aspirations they had had for their daughter, obliterated in the span of a second They were devastated at their daughter's loss and with 4 young children to raise alone. How was she going to cope with the huge responsibility that had landed on her head It was a huge unforeseen tragedy in which fate had dealt their daughter a cruel blow.

A blow so violent that she may never be able to recover from it. This tragedy would have irreversible consequences not only for their daughter but for the entire family.

Where were her children? Andromeda glanced around furtively to see where those poor mites were. Probably skulking away in corners, shying away from the keen curious stares of all these strange faces.

In the last 48 hours their lives had been turned upside down, in a single heartbeat shattering their dreams and hopes for the future. The father who had been at the peak of good health had promised them many adventures once he was back Instead he had come home to them in a sealed casket.

Seeing him lying there in his eternal sleep, oblivious to the piercing cries of mourning and lamenting all around him his prone, inert form belied the vivid boisterous man that had once been. The image would be seared onto their young minds from that very moment Andromeda prayed for her children that night in all her earnestness and deep seated anguish her grief knowing no bounds. She asked God to protect them from the nightmares and the harsh reality that awaited them all without her husband. She felt like the walls of despondency were closing in on her. She had to keep it together. This was no time to fall apart

* * *

CHAPTER 20

ANDROMEDA

"I am now a widow and my children fatherless. A word many women dread to become. How on earth was I going to cope? I know nothing about the outside world and how to provide sustenance for my family. My husband took over every aspect of life, and shielded me from the practicalities of life outside the home. I see in my visions a long dark road, stretched out ahead of me, the blackness terrifying and engulfing, the stench of death drawing closer, I could already feel it gnawing away at me, as my skin prickled in terror at the fate that lay before me. The beast that fed off my fears was here, upon me ready to rip me to shreds and tear me to pieces." The path that now lies before me bears only insurmountable obstacles, hurdles I alone cannot cross without falling into. How do I take those first few steps into the unknown, where only an endless void of uncertainties awaits. Can I do this alone? I ask myself for the thousandth time. He is no longer here to hold my hand and help me navigate the turbulent waters of life.

Andromeda knew she would face stigma at every corner when in Pakistan. The hurdles and resistance that were waiting to greet her as she tried to integrate back into society were going to appear in full force. It was all waiting for her. A society that evidently had no room for women like her. Maybe she was being a little too pessimistic, she thought, back tracking on her thoughts, perhaps she was panicking a little too much. The world had advanced and it could be that society and even the culture of her parents and her in laws had become more accommodating. As a widowed woman, she would find sympathy, support and understanding. She was being absurd to think that there were people out there who thought otherwise. There was good and bad everywhere, but for the most part, she was confident that people would treat her with compassion and gradually help her back on her feet if they could

* * *

CHAPTER 21

THE GLOVES ARE OFF

Andromeda approached everyone tentatively, walking on eggshells. She felt that all eyes were upon her trying to discern her every move ready to wade in with their judgements Feeling herself exposed and deeply vulnerable, she teetered precariously on a tightrope of uncertainty. Her shattered life, now lay before her scattered in pieces like her heart. She was surrounded by people who were now unmasked and unyielding in their contempt towards her. In the years that had passed, she had never fit in due to her inability to mould her mindset to theirs She had laboured in isolation but nothing she ever did was good enough

Andromeda had always pondered why widowers were never stigmatised in the way that widows were. Divorced women were also perceived as a stigma, a blot on society, and to be avoided at all costs.

It was not as if the widows had brought about the untimely demise of their husbands or had any influence or control in their deaths. They could not have prevented their husband's death had they tried.

Now the accusations hung menacingly in the air. The body of her husband was barely cold in its grave when the vultures had begun circling around.

The omens had been there all along, but she had been too naive and too absent, caught up in her punishing household regimen to take note.

* * *

CHAPTER 22

PREDATORS LET THE GAMES BEGIN

Her mother-in-law, was a formidable woman and the central commanding figure in these closeted meets. Andromeda learned only after becoming a widow that she had known very little about the man she had married, and who had fathered her children. They had never discussed the practicalities of life after death, wills and probates, inheritance. It had remained a close topic and off limits. This often infuriated her, but there was very little she could do.

Any mere mention of such things triggered a rage and anger in her husband. He had always remained cagey about such matters, she had thought wearily. Their constant arguments and feuding had remained at the heart of their marriage, in part due to their conflicting opinions and the other part attributed to her in laws' dismissive views towards her. It had been nothing less than a rollercoaster marriage.

To her it was a normal enough thing for a couple to discuss, plan and make future preparations for the security of the children. Isn't that what marriage was all about, she thought the sanctity and protection of one's family was central in every relationship. It was the ultimate goal in any marriage. Provision and future security were of paramount importance as was love Andromeda reasoned to herself. It took away the uncertainties in case of the unforeseeable events such as death of a family member. It was never. And thing to be unprepared

The only problem was that such talks or any talk with her husband had been hijacked and often vetted by her in-laws. They held sway over everything that took place in the home. Most of all the influence over Andromeda's husband was apparent in the way he rejected her offerings at every turn. To him she was immature and unimportant where family discussions were concerned.

Her in laws were very careful and took pains to shield her from their talks with her husband. Over the years, this had become an established pattern, and she continued to live in a state of ignorance, her husband had grown distant over time, which was no surprise, considering the influence he was under. He had rarely ever shared anything with his wife.

She would come to learn more about her husband in death than she ever did in life as one by one the secrets came to light.

* * *

CHAPTER 23

NO HOLDING BACK – DRAWN KNIVES

The knives were out. Distribution of assets was at the forefront of their minds. The grieving process had been short-lived and all too soon forgotten, as her in laws set about making plans to secure the lands.

They had been so preoccupied with their mission to wrestle control of Andromeda's husband's assets that they had been blissfully unaware of the suspicious glances cast their way as the other guests watched in stunned disbelief their antics, darting sympathetic glances Andromeda's way.

She had not known much about her husband's finances as he had never talked about it with her in detail. He was always evasive and if she had persisted, it only resulted in angering him further. So much for equality, Andromeda had thought resentfully. They were a couple and parents to 4 beautiful children, what secrets would they keep from one another. They were a team or so she had thought.

A wife's role was one of dutiful obedience, to serve and not question her husband's affairs. Financial matters rested only with the husband. No questions asked. This was the unspoken rule of patriarchy

She was given money for housekeeping each month which was a paltry amount and barely stretched to buying food and groceries. For the rest her husband had always managed the finances himself, providing things for his wife and children as and when needed.

Andromeda did find it highly implausible and often demeaning, to ask for money to buy food. It was soul destroying not to mention stripping her of very shred of dignity at having no control over her life and being completely dependent.

It chipped away at her layers of confidence, and self-esteem, she felt utterly useless and dependant on her husband for everything. It was a galling feeling.

Andromeda' mother in law was a highly superstitious woman in her 70s, very sharp, and with a mind as astute as someone half her age. Nothing however escaped her. Andromeda felt she was under continuous scrutiny.

Any notions that Andromeda ever had of being independent and empowering herself with skills and knowledge had long been buried and put to rest by her husband and her in-laws.

It came as no great surprise that Andromeda's cluelessness and lack of information regarding her husband's assets proved to be highly advantageous for her in-laws.

The sprawling acres of lush agricultural land which stretched as far as the eye could see, and worth their weight in gold would be easy to take and restored back into their hands where they belonged. The children were too young, and what would they know of such matters anyway.

They would turn out just like their wayward and useless mother. Andromeda's mother in law scoffed with disdain at the thought of her daughter in law becoming empowered and taking ownership of her late son's assets. Why did her son have to die and not this wench who had brought nothing but grief to this family, she thought with barely suppressed rage, She spat out a mouthful of cane that she had been chewing on.

Andromeda had never doubted for a second that she in laws disliked, her mother in law was very vocal about it too, continuously in her son's ear about his wife's shortfalls. She considered Andromeda to be the worst mistake to have ever darkened their doors. A mistake that would have far reaching repercussions for her impeccable son. It was never too late for her son to get rid of his wife, of course and remarry again. Of course they had already put the notion in his head. He had protested citing his 4 children as the reason, but he was not completely opposed to the idea, her mother in law noted with satisfaction.

There were so many better and prettier options than Andromeda out there. In no time at all, they would find a suitable bride for their son. He was still quite eligible and of course he could take the children and let Andromeda go.
She had borne these insults with a heavy aching heart. She turned to prayer for the taunting and threats to stop. They were relentless and had worn her down.

Her marriage was teetering on the brink of a precipice as it was. It would be so easy for her husband to succumb to his families' wishes and be rid of her once and for all. To top it all he had his parents' blessings.

Life had other plans...

Little did he suspect that on the day of December 20th his life would come to an end, a hidden heart condition had claimed him in his sleep the day he was due to fly back to his wife and children.

* * *

CHAPTER 24

THE LANDS

She was completely ignorant on the workings of her husband's land. Her mother in law, and sister in laws gathered in the corner of the unlit courtyard. The distant chatter of relatives could be heard from the rooms opposite the veranda, electricity was in short supply, so light from the oil lamps cast shadows which danced wildly on the roofs and clay baked walls, casting the many huddled bodies in an eerie light.

These lands had been in the family for generations and as the head son of the family, her son now gone and his surviving brother had controlled it. Now it would be Andromeda's son who was the rightful heir to his father's lands and once he was old enough they were his to do as he saw fit.

Her mother-in-law had balked at the idea. She would not allow this to happen, Andromeda could not be trusted with anything, she was a reckless, cause, an immature woman, her mother in law declared as her daughters agreed vociferously. The oldest and allegedly the shrewdest of Andromeda's sister in laws pointed out that Andromeda would have many sympathisers who would want to see justice done for the grieving widow and her young children.

To prevent other opportunists and well-meaning busy bodies getting to her, they had to act fast, she warned. In Andromeda's currant stricken state she would be more pliable to coerce in handing over her consent, lock, stock, and barrel to all that her husband owned, if they played their cards right, everything that belonged to his heirs would be in their hands.

No time to lose, now that they had buried her husband following an elaborate ceremony in which hundreds of mourners had turned out to watch him laid to rest in the family plot, Andromeda's in laws put into motion their plans from the night before.

It was now or never, Andromeda could not walk away with the rights to the estate intact unless they staged a subtle intervention. One in which she unknowingly handed over everything to them until it was too late to retract her decision.

While she was in her pathetically numb state of wretchedness, shock and apparent confusion, it would be easy to get her compliance, they had agreed in the early hours last night, when most of the guests were asleep, her in laws were deep in muted conversation, occasionally throwing glances at the room which Andromeda shared with her parents and a couple of her husband's aunties.

Once the last of the guests had departed, her brother-in-law, now made the unofficially declared head of the family, was the youngest amongst his siblings but also sorely lacking in intellect, mannerisms and diplomacy. He had made Andromeda's life miserable for years, spring boarding off the coattails of his older more distinguished brother, exploiting his entitled status of being the youngest sibling in the family. His own mother was susceptible to his demands, therefore gaining leverage with his older brother was a cakewalk, he was indulged, pampered and spoilt to a fault. That had not been enough as he created rifts between his brother and Andromeda on many occasions, revelling in the fights that ensued between the couple.

Now clutching a sheaf of papers his mother had given him, he went to seek out his sister-in-law. They had not spoken much since she had arrived distraught and dishevelled from the long journey in which Andromeda had been heavily sedated as she had not been fit to take the journey otherwise.

The funeral preparations and attending to the large volume of guests had preoccupied him. He had never held Andromeda in much esteem, and had never made any bones about his dislike for her either. He just could not understood what his older brother ever saw in her. It was baffling.

She was plain, and average and dull witted as his family had also unanimously agreed. His handsome brother with his immaculate charm, sharp wit and unmatched credentials could have chosen someone far better and prettier. Hopefully they could get rid of her, take the kids and be done with it.

She was so stupid she would not even know what they were asking of her, hopefully tonight, she would sign the papers and his family would be immensely rich and much better off for it. The lands were of no use to the foolish woman anyway he thought scornfully Getting the lands back, meant he would have a lion's share of the wealth. It was a win-win situation for him, and his family, as he chuckled to himself. Andromeda did not deserve a dime as far as he and his mother were concerned Let her parents take care of her and her children She was no longer their problem His brother was gone and she did not belong here anymore.

* * *

CHAPTER 25

HUGE RED FLAG

The first red flag which sprung up in Andromeda's mind was the evening when her brother-in-law clutching a sheet of papers, approached her, totally dismissive of his sister-in-law's bereft state, announced that she had to sign some papers and accompany him at first light to the registrar's office for some official paperwork.

Thankfully, Andromeda had not been as unhinged as they would have liked to see, for her faculties were still about her. She refused, stunned at the audacity but not surprised that they had wasted no time in moving in to relieve her of her children's inheritance, thinking she was too aggrieved to notice.

The audacity and barefaced cheek of their assumptions, she thought indignantly. Obviously they credited her with far less intelligence than she thought. They had actually counted on the fact that they would be able to get away unimpeded and unchallenged by Andromeda. Amidst her grieving state, she had not abandoned her faculties entirely. Clearly they thought she posed no threat to their nefarious schemes.

They could not have been more wrong, Andromeda thought, determinedly. She would see about that. From now on, she would have to be sharp, and on her guard, ready for anything.

The cloak of protection her late husband had provided her was now gone, and buried 6 feet deep. She had to be smart and keep her wits about her. A rising sense of dread and panic which she struggled to keep down told her that, her in-laws were out for the kill. They had no reason or qualms about taking her under their wing now. She had never been welcome amongst them, but a liability. Now she could go and drop dead for all they cared. The person who had mattered and had been the sole reason for linking them together was now gone, they had no allegiance to their brother's wife. She was in effect nobody to them .They had never like her much anyway, she had always been a misfit within their family.

* * *

CHAPTER 26

THE CHALEESWAH – 40 DAYS

In the village, Andromeda had to sit out the 40-day mourning period, which was not a mandatory practice or even a tradition. The normal rule of convention for mourning in Islamic culture was 3 days. Here however in this remote village of the Punjab, the family adhered to their own self constructed beliefs.

The relatives had a field day gossiping and throwing searching glances her way. There was not much Andromeda could do about that, she thought, wryly suppressing an impatient sigh. They were simply not worth her getting stressed over especially as there was little she could do to sway them. She had more important things to contend with right now She could not let them affect her given her fragile disposition and delicate state of mind However knowing them as she did it was doubtless they would not attempt to cause her further anguish they had no sympathy for her and her children.

In one fatal blow death had shown her how it could strike at any time without warning. An inevitable reality for every person, death hung and hovered in the shadows waiting expectantly to claim its next victim, like the sword of Damocles waiting in earnest to deliver its final blow. She learnt first-hand that day how life could be taken away, with such ease, snuffed out like a lowly flame, leaving only the void of grief and darkness for those left behind. The aftershocks continued to come, rising and falling in waves.

* * *

CHAPTER 27

OPEN SECRET

Her husband had been a man who had lived and breathed life in whatever he did. He had many friends and there was never a dull moment to be had for him. It was a merry go round of activities, the buzz of entertainment and being entertained.

Whilst Andromeda languished painstakingly at home in the kitchen, cooking meals for his large contingent of family members, cleaning and doing the chores that never seemed to end, her husband was out all hours after work. Once he had napped in the afternoon, he took himself off to the squash courts built in the leisure facility within the compound only a few blocks away. It was an excellent way to let off steam and forget about work for a bit.

Though he was not an athletically driven man or a fitness fanatic by any means like some of his colleagues, he liked to indulge in the few leisurely pursuit's for instance walking, golf, and squash. On long, balmy summer nights he loved to meet up with friends at the army mess for a late night's session of billiards and cards.

One of his closest friends was Dawood. He was single and with far less responsibilities He loved to live it up on the weekends enjoying the single life and free from any domestic obligations. In his spare time he loved to dabble on the stock market perusing the internet for the latest market trends and make the odd investments where a potential profit caught his keen eye. It was the one weekend that Andromeda recalled when her husband had promised to take her out Instead he had forgotten it had been their wedding anniversary and they were going to go out for dinner to celebrate He had gone out to the army mess around late afternoon to meet his friend. They had ended up losing all track of time as they played billiards and sat around with other members present at the club Oblivious to the early hours of the morning as the first threads of dawn began to appear Andromeda's husband and Dawood had continued to play undeterred by the lateness of the hour even though the other men had long since retired to their beds.

His wife would be fast asleep anyway he thought he did not have to feel guilty he thought to himself he would take her out some other day Her job was in the home to take care of his family and the children He did enough for them anyway he reasoned

The fact that she spent all her waking hours cooking, cleaning, and overseeing the demands of a continuous stream of guests that never stopped arriving had slipped his consciousness She was only doing what her duty as a traditional wife entailed and anyway his family helped out in the home he was sure of it. They had been nothing if not accommodating and helpful to his wife. To him they could do no wrong

In any period of adjustment there were always bound to be teething problems His wife was young immature and at times he thought that she was very stupid but given time she would mould herself into their culture and acquire their methods He was blessed that he had a good family who would lookout for his wife and help her at each hurdle.

She had a lot to learn. Although the fact that his family were treating his wife appallingly behind the scenes and setting her up to fail had escaped his attention. It would never have occurred to him given the deep trust he held for his parents and siblings Andromeda's complaints to him had appeared to be delusional fabrications of her immature mind he had told himself She was far too sensitive and took everything personally Andromeda's concerns fell upon deaf ears her in laws had played it so well until now, they had been very clever to avoid getting caught Her husband would never come to know the real sinister truth behind the facade of pleasantries they posed.

Andromeda's husband was blissfully ignorant to his wife's unhappiness and loneliness. It had gotten to a point that he deliberately chose to avoid spending hours at home where nagging family members constantly unleashed a barrage of complaints and the atmosphere in general was stifling.

His wife had been unhappy for a long time but he solely blamed her for not fitting in and appeasing his family. Even her long silences were a testament to her weak character he thought angrily. If she did speak out then she sounded like the immature, uncultured fool that she was, a little girl whining and complaining to him about his family. He acknowledged they had their moments, but he was blinded to many of their faults and in his eyes they could do now wrong. Andromeda was just being petulant, and childish, and her paranoia about his family was getting on his nerves. There was no way his family would treat his wife in the way she described to him often. She was far too sensitive for her own good, he thought letting out an exasperated sigh.

* * *

CHAPTER 28

FEUDING INTENSIFIED

Andromeda always struggled to understand why one set of parents had the monopoly over the other. From the start there had always existed a rivalry leading to unhealthy competition between her in laws and her parents. It was bizarre. Although related, both existed in different worlds and had very little exposure to one another. The alliance brought by the marriage of Andromeda and their son could have enhanced and nurtured those bonds further had they chosen to do so. Unfortunately, much to Andromeda's detriment, illiteracy and closeted mindsets prevailed leading to raging conflicts and bitter feuds, for no other reason than the fact that Andromeda's in-laws wanted to exact superiority and allude to an unshakeable dominance over everyone else.

This meant an increasing exchange of hostilities over the years, propounded by their actions, harsh words, accusations all aimed at Andromeda's parents, but unleashed upon her at every opportunity. There was no need for it, except that it hurt her to the very core to hear slander against her parents, her family being vilified, and her own lack of experience and struggle to adapt to their environment added to her despair. She could not fight back in defence for to do so meant she was laying herself wide open for more abuse.

However, it was commendable Andromeda thought, that despite the glaring absence of literacy and opportunities for women especially in her in-laws village, they had thought it important to educate their eldest son. They had large acres of land which was cultivated and managed by hired village hands, but for a large family, it was still a struggle. Patriarchy from generations gone had left its mark to present day, and it was deemed apt to award special privileges and benefits to the men of the house. Women in general aside from the matriarch of the family had very little input. To speak out was inviting disaster upon her own head.

From the depths of poverty and hardship they had made provisions for the education of her husband and had sent him to the finest school there was in another district. Although money had always been scarce and resources scant, he had excelled in all his studies working hard from an incredibly young age much to his parent's great relief.

They had lived in the jaws of poverty for many years despite having swathes of agricultural land, it had still proved to be a struggle as good harvests were not always predicted especially in the scorching summer months when temperatures exceed 50 degrees or in the monsoon seasons when battering deluges obliterated the freshly sown crops It was always a gamble against the temperamental climate.

They counted their blessings as in many ways they were better off than most of the villagers and relatives who lived a meagre existence. Andromeda's husband was an ambitious young man, driven and motivated to turn his family's fortunes around which would eventually set him on the path to success. He wanted to give them a good life as they had pooled everything into ensuring he received a good education Most young men in his social group wanted to party and mess around and settle for any job that ensured a pay check at the end as long as it paid the bills and put food on the table

The family were strongly set in their ways, with entrenched beliefs and rigid norms. They were in fact very old school as was he. Despite having travelled far and wide, more than any of his family members who had never seen a plane much less travelled on one, Andromeda's husband remained firmly rooted to the traditions that had borne out of his childhood home. Andromeda had no issue with the culture or traditions in general that her roots were borne from, but it was the harsh customary practices, and deep seated conservatism she came to face in which she clashed with her in-laws.

A woman who had come from another country, another culture, despite being a relative was unused to their way of living,unschooled and unprepared for the harshness of life in Pakistan. The mindsets were completely different, Andromeda found that she had become nothing more than a mere liability.

She was expected to toe the line and ask no questions. Her role as a young wife, mother and daughter in law were to obey and remain submissive at all times if she was to survive in her marital home.

On the other hand her husband had been brought up to understand that male dominance held the highest rank in all matters, females were assigned a much lower rank in his estimation. They had very little say in everyday matters without the notable exception of his mother who brandished her own weapon of authority. She was the commander in chief that ruled the house with an iron will and no one including her children could make a dent in her indomitable stance.

* * *

CHAPTER 29

NO WIN

She could not win either way had she tried. They were a family impossible to please. He was not happy either for this preconceived marriage that had been arranged in haste, but they had to make the most of it for the children they had created together.

He was a man with an undeterred ambition to become financially wealthy, and nothing and no one was going to stop him. His work was one thing, but continuously plotting and planning and eking out opportunities as a side hustle dominated his thoughts day and night. They rarely communicated with one another, Andromeda had never felt so alone in her marriage. They had got to a point that little was spoken between them, both had withdrawn inadvertently, and were just going through the motions as family.

Her husband had put little emphasis on planning for the unforeseeable future. Career progression and promotion had dominated his thought processes day and night. She often heard him from the bathroom reciting speeches to himself that he had memorised. His career was everything to him as were his children. Both were exclusive to each other.

As stress piled on in layers, even to the detriment of his own health, he had ignored the warnings, neither had he shared what could have been significant information to his wife. There were so many what ifs, she bemoaned .There were so many questions swimming around in her head What had her husband kept from her all these years Had he harboured some secret illness that he never told her of Had he been trying to protect her Now she would never know the answers to any of these. All these years together and yet she was only just discovering that she had barely known her husband at all.

She could have staged an intervention, helped him, they could have embarked upon a life plan together with healthier choices and alleviated the stress workload together. If only, but his male pride and ego, and the yawning distance that had appeared in their marriage had all but rendered it impossible.

What could she have done to prevent it? She asked herself this question a hundred times. In reality, over time, her husband had become his own worst enemy, especially regarding his health. Ultimately, he ended up paying a huge price for this lapse. Death had claimed him in the prime of his life, when all his carefully laid plans and ambitions for a future turned to the dust of nothingness.

He had lived a life of very little excesses and guarded his health fiercely. Stress may have been a mitigating factor as Andromeda had seen close up, her husband's complex relationships with all his extended family, pummelled by all sides with score settling, administering advice, settling disputes. She too had been caught up in the web of conflict and hostilities, from the moment she had set foot in the country. Many of these conflicts had taken root and expanded into large scale open warfare mostly engineered by her in laws. They seemed to find no qualms in causing chaos and dissension among the wider ranks of family Did they get a buzz or a rush out of deploying such tactics? Andromeda wondered with puzzlement

She had witnessed people reduced to tears and protesting innocence at the accusatory claims hurled at them and the unjustified aspersions her in laws cast in their wide net. She had witnessed families who had been inseparable and close with each other go to war over petty disputes that had escalated over time. Seeing it all first-hand she had noted the derision and mocking by her in-laws as they revelled in their shallow victories.

Family structures destroyed and estrangements that spanned years of not talking ensued in their wake as they were pitted against each other. It had become a way of life for Andromeda's in laws. The one fascinating feature which bordered on the bizarre extreme was their uncanny ability to forge ties with families they had been instrumental in breaking up, practicing diplomacy with great aplomb and in the process relegating themselves to a position of respectable superiority in the wide spread family. Though many knew of their sly intentions and had woken up to their ill-concealed intentions there were still a good few who would never have suspected for an instance that they had created havoc in the first instance. It was conflict at its best Andromeda thought wryly.

* * *

CHAPTER 30

COMPLIANCE

She would have felt a tiny smidge of sympathy for her husband had it not been for his unwitting stubbornness to resist standing up to their injustices. More often than she cared to remember, she had borne the brunt of his family's wrath, relatives, of her in-laws and therefore hers by genealogy. Though they were all closely related, her aunts, uncles, cousins and their respective offspring, to Andromeda they may as well have been total strangers as she had never met them or gotten to know them having lived for most of her young life in the UK.

She was new to the country, to their way of life, to traditional and cultural practices, yet this had not deterred them from having a field day in throwing in their lot with the plethora of condescending criticisms and scathing comments. She was a total misfit and stood out like the school idiot as, every word and sentence rained down upon her day in day out, eroding and stripping away her self-esteem and confidence.

On many occasions Andromeda had hoped and prayed that her husband would man up to all these people who were virtual strangers to her and take a protective stance. Wasn't that what most husbands were meant to do for their spouse? For better for worse, in sickness and health until death do we part?

Her husband, a man torn between his career, his marriage and children, and the continuous demands of relations, spring boarding off whether it was to find some poor lowly relation employment, or provide bed and lodgings to relations seeking sympathy and whatever they could muster out of him, he was in popular demand.

What galled Andromeda was that he willingly bore the stress to the point of jeopardising his own well-being and peace of mind, and he had allowed the advances of his opportunistic relations to cast a pall over their marriage. Irritations, fights and quarrels flared up inevitably. Not a day went by when Andromeda had not had cause to despair. She could not even recall when there had been consecutive days when they had been allowed to live in tranquil marital bliss.

The marriage had been hijacked from day one by her husband's unruly family. In name only she was his wife and the bearer of his children. The rest was determined and managed by the whims and authoritative powers of Andromeda's mother-in-law.

Despite the slow agonising years of hostilities, and conflict fuelled days. Andromeda had survived the brunt of what many would have taken to their heels and run. She had known that options were far less and limited to a woman in her situation.

A proud and doting father who lived with the dreams of watching his children grow up, graduate, get married and have children. He was yet to experience the indescribable joys of being a grandfather and savouring the untold bliss of holding his precious grandchildren and playing with them.

During many of their conversations he had been very enigmatic about the future as he told his wife, this was what he ultimately strove for. In all the years of toil and hardship grandchildren would be his greatest achievements. It was a tragedy of many sorts, when he had reached the pinnacle of a fine prestigious career spanning 4 decades, he had been in the offing for a senior high-ranking promotion.

The peak of his glorious career and the long hard years of study, training and toil were about to be paid off, the ultimate reward and acknowledgement of diligent service to his nation and its people displayed by the rank awaiting to be conferred upon him upon his return to his country.

Fate however had other plans in store and none of them involved returning home to his family as he had once been. A vivacious, son of standing rank and honour, a man who made, many a dream come true. The born leader who served as a patriarchal figure of authority in his home, a man who was topped to become a high ranking Chief. Everything that he had once been and was topped to become, no longer was present. Like his soul, his dreams too, his plans the lofty ambitions he had held dear had departed and only those fleeting memories of the man he had been now remained.

* * *

CHAPTER 31

ILLITERACY IN THE RANKS

She saw three of her sisters-in-law bustling about with utensils, overseeing preparations for food and blankets, helped by cousins. As they shouted out instructions to the helpers and hands milling about in a fog of confusion, her mother-in-law mingled amongst the throng of village women who had been there all day, and some only loitered for the sake of satisfying their curiosity and sense of gossip.

For it was on such occasions like these, be they weddings or funerals in the village where, gossip was rampant like the wind; it blew whichever way the wind direction was. They looked her way, Andromeda noticed, with unreadable expressions and she could not help but feel they were anything but comforting or sympathetic vibes that emanated forth.

There was an unmistakeable sense of barely controlled hostility in the air, perhaps she was imagining things. But her 6th sense nagged away at her. It was apparent because no one from her in-laws including her mother-in-law had once approached or looked her way. They were all grieving but they were grieving apart.

She spotted her children. It broke her heart to see how bereft and stricken they were in their unexpressed grief. Her older child, Samuel , who was barely 15 but far more wise beyond his years. He sat submerged in his grief, as Andromeda's parents consoled him, hugging him and whispering comforting words to the boy who sat in the shaded veranda, shoulders slumped and head dropped to his chest in utter wretchedness.

The strength her beautiful boy had shown and dignity in his own grief whilst taking care of his mother during the arduous journey from Beijing, made her aching heart swell with pride, love, joy and pain, pain at the irreplaceable loss of a father her children would suffer for the rest of their lives.

Her daughters were in pain, all she wanted to do was to take her 4 children and clasp them tightly to her chest and she would never let them go. She would fight to bring the light of joy back into their aching broken hearts. She could only offer them love and her all, but she could not sadly bring back their father.

Her little one sat with her, uncomprehending and curious, as he watched all these strange people gathered in this place. Her sweet little son, he was barely 3 years old, and had only gotten to spend too little time with his father. Andromeda recalled with a fresh surge of tears cascading down her cheeks at how delighted her husband had been upon learning he had another son

Now their family was complete - two boys and two girls. She would never forget how smitten her husband had been every time he looked at his youngest child. The love was indescribable He had been an amazing father and each of his children were special to him and they'll knew that for they in turn loved him dearly. He had celebrated joyously upon the arrival of his fourth child making plans for the future.

Everywhere they went he carried his young son close to him Smiling and laughing at his baby antics. Her other children were also delighted by the latest addition to their family a little baby brother Overall the last 3 years had been a glorious time of fond memories with her husband and her children. She had never seen her husband so happy and as a family for once they were all in a good place Andromeda thought. The happiness however proved to be only short lived.

As Andromeda's tears fell silently down her cheeks, she had felt many times the sensation of two tiny soft hands creep up around her neck gently and place them over her eyes, their touch cooling the sting and the burning sensation in them from the countless tears she had shed.

Her precious little boy could not speak but his actions told her what his little heart felt but could not articulate. His mother's pain could be felt but not explained. She ached for all her precious children who were going to grow up without the comforting presence of their father through life.

They would feel his absence notably at every milestone and juncture of both successes and failures. The empty void he had left would be an ever-present burden of pain which they all would carry throughout their adult lives.

Grief was not something that went away or diminished but somehow they had to adapt and acknowledge it, difficult as it was going to be. Pain, tragedy, losing loved ones was a lesson that they had begun to learn from early on in their lives. Sadly, there was not much Andromeda could do for them except love and support them through their long journey of grief.

* * *

CHAPTER 32

SHINING STAR

When nightfall eventually came and the last of the villagers had retired to their homes, the family moved to the inside quarters. The night was still young. To Andromeda, it felt like 10 years and passed in the space of a few hours.

As the dying embers in the clay hearths began to fade, tinging the air with the acrid smell of burning wood, the beds, charpois had been moved inside. She held her little boy who was nestled in the crook of her arms, and he was talking in his usual mono syllabic word sentences. When he asked her, where was Papa, it took the last remaining vestiges of self-control for her not to break down as Andromeda explained pointing up at the sky with her index finger, her son followed his mother's gaze as she told him that his father was right up there in the vast sky, its inky blackness decorated with a palette of twinkling stars.

Father had been summoned by God to go to another world, a distant planet, she told her wide-eyed boy who listened earnestly, intrigue and wonder reflected in his huge brown eyes as he absorbed his mother's soothing words.

To a two-year-old who knew nothing, and was with the with the blissful innocence of babies, he readily accepted his mother's soft sweet explanation that God had turned his father into this amazing Super Star hero, and once father's work was done, they would all be reunited like one big happy family once more. There were people in all those other distant far off planets and shimmering worlds where he was greatly needed she explained to her fascinated son.

His father was a superhero, not just any a star. He had magical powers that helped people who lived on other planets like he did. Then sleep overtook her little boy, as she closed her eyes tightly feeling the hot prickling tears fall.

Andromeda spoke softly and gently as her son's eyelids began to grow heavy, with sleep. He snuggled closer into the comforting warmth of her chest. The last words he heard before drifting off was his mother's gentle voice telling him that whenever he missed his father, each day he could summon him in his dreams. It was a magical place and they could be anything they wanted there She told him in soft soothing tones as she gazed adoringly at the sleeping form of her child cradled in her arms that his father would be watching over all of them and one day they would all be together again.

It took a great vestige of control for Andromeda not to buckle under grief. She needed to conjure up something to her son to cushion the blow she knew would come for her 2-year-old in the years ahead.

For now her words were but a band aid to his little precious soul.

* * *

CHAPTER 33

THE ELDEST SON

Her older son had felt the blow of his father's death more keenly, and in the short space of time they had received the news and travelled miles, something had hardened in his soul, a lump of sorrow, as grief and anger choked him. It was unfair - why his father, and why now? He needed his father, they had made plans, plans that had not involved his father leaving him so soon.

There had been much work to be done and he didn't know as the rising sobs gave way to quiet silent convulsions, the tears fell followed by more, refusing to lessen, in their intensity. He felt powerless, helpless, looking across at the silent hunched figure of his mother, head bowed, and sat quietly in one corner of the covered courtyard, as everyone else milled about her - all he could see was a broken woman, lost without her husband.

It was as if he had to bid farewell to his childhood of 15 years and assume the mantle of the eldest in his family. His mother was a wreck and his young siblings had not known what had hit them and were struggling to understand the gravity of losing their father. Their lives had been turned upside down. He was hurting and in so much pain but one look at the slumped defeated form of his mother cradling his baby brother, hardened his resolve. He had to take care of his broken family.

* * *

CHAPTER 34

NEW NORMAL

That same evening everyone congregated to the big room as loud raucous laughter and shouts rang out into the stillness of the evening. They sang traditional tunes and made merry as they hurled teasing remarks at one another across the room. Meanwhile his own kin, celebrated unabashedly without remorse or reservation oblivious to the pain of their brother's widow sat with her children in the next room. It was adjoined by 2 small concrete steps and accessible through a pair of shuttered rickety doors from where she could observe their antics and tried in vain to block out their raucous laughter.

She wanted to scream and lay bare her raw grief at the injustice of it all, but she couldn't and wouldn't make a spectacle of herself. Her grief was raw and palpable eating her up from within. At this moment in time no-one could fathom the consuming sensation of being encased in a prison of pain from which there seemed no escape. She was drowning in sorrow and felt the pain sear through her insides like a cold knife of steel. Undoubtedly her mother in law would be experiencing far worse, consumed in her sorrow, ripped apart by grief so unimaginable that Andromeda's heart went out to her. No mother should ever have to bury their child. It was not the natural order of things.

It was unimaginable to think of for Andromeda thought no parent should have to bury their child It went against the laws of nature If only their hearts were not hardened towards her she ventured forth to console her mother in law only to be brushed aside roughly by her sister in laws who kept a close vigil around their grief stricken mother Their eyes glistened with anger as she had tried to approach until finally she had given up and retreated back to where her parents sat looking distressed and heartbroken at their daughter's turn in fortune It was hard to believe that their young daughter was now a widow. The thought tore at their insides Fate could be so cruel

They were incapable of understanding, plus her children could not be a witness to her meltdown, these little souls were hurting and she had to first help repair their injured hearts and for that she could put all her anger and emotion aside.

It wasn't so much the lack of respect for the dead, or the blatant disregard for Andromeda's feelings, but it was the other grieving relatives who were stopping over, unable to sleep, rest or say anything. They were met with derision and scorn if they dared to voice a complaint. They huddled beneath the coarse patchwork "Razais"

They continued their antics into the early hours of the night vying to be heard above the cacophony of each other's voices as the sounds of their loud laughter reached the few women housed in the farther most room across the courtyard, through the metal grills of the windows. Silent tears rolled down Andromeda's cheeks as she lay on her side, facing the wall, with her face resting on both hands Andromeda lay still and motionless like a cold stone statue feeling devoid and empty inside. She listened to the sounds of merriment and loud boisterous voices wafting in from across the courtyard carried through to her on this the cold night sky, a contrast to the misery and grief enveloping her.

Her husband now lay 6 feet under severed from all connection of the earthly world

She choked back another wave of sobs that threatened to engulf her as she felt the world imploding all around her.
Mercifully Andromeda managed to succumb to her exhausted state and fell into a deep sleep. Plagued by nightmarish visions, she had tossed and turned, and each time she had opened her eyes to grasp the reality of her situation, she had cried herself back to sleep.

Such was the sorry life of a person, in life he had reigned in all of their hearts their hearts, and in death he was all but forgotten. His first night in his cold dark grave underneath the stars, he lay, all alone consigned to the eternal sleep of many who had passed before him and many who were sure to follow. This was life coming full circle ashes to ashes, dust to dust the ultimate end. Through his children her husband would live on his spirit would continue to prevail through his progeny, Andromeda consoled herself

Her in-laws had not ventured to console her children or offer Andromeda some words of comfort. The link between her and them was lying in a cold grave a few yards away from the house. That link was now broken and to them she was nobody but a mere inconvenience.

How could they be so jovial and happy and switch off their grief in an instant. Were the last two days' spectacle put on for show and it had barely been less than 48 hours since they had laid her husband to rest? Maybe it was their way of dealing with the aftermath of a tragedy which undoubtedly was to affect the lives of everybody present. Who knew what was going through each of their minds?

After all he had been the patriarch and go-to person for all of their sorry troubles.

Andromeda observed all this silently wrapped in her thoughts and implications that loomed before her, raising her children without a father being her main concern.

The last thread of daylight had all but disappeared and the open dark sky loomed above like a blanket of black velvet stretching as far as the eyes could see. An impressive conglomeration of stars sprinkled across its broad expanse, twinkling and glittering far away, like sparkling sequins.

The sky was very clear that night and even the moon and stars were out in full force today paying tribute to a great soul. She sat for a while as everyone else had moved indoors. It had become cooler following the scorching temps of the day. The pleasant feel of the nightly breeze comforted Andromeda as she sat there alone cradling her son. The heady fragrance of jasmine wafted from the trees nearby, enveloping her in its sweet hypnotic embrace.

The courtyard now empty, yawned like a big empty mouth strewn with the littered remains of the day, where her husband had lain in his mortal sleep, on display for the hundreds of people who had thronged in their united grief.

Now everything was silent except for the occasional smattering of bird noise, shutters banging shut from neighbouring homes. The sounds of livestock tethered in courtyards adjoining the house pierced the air with their cries, and grunts and the bellowing roars of buffaloes tied up in their shelters, added to the orchestras of sound.

Like the people who had thronged here in their hordes, united in their grief, the animals had seemed to sense it and were restless from the excitement of it all.

Andromeda sat alone with her thoughts, silent tears cascaded down her gaunt pale face. Every so often she could hear laughter erupting from inside the shuttered rooms once she had shared with her husband each time they had come to stay for the holidays.

All around here, the memories came thick and fast, she could see him so clearly in his white starched cotton suit he preferred to wear in the summer, walking around the courtyard of his home, sleek black hair a direct contrast to his attire. He had one of those personas that could light up a room and dazzle people with his down to earth nature. He never differentiated between those who were on a lower socio-economic scale but went to great lengths to help the impoverished in his village. He had been regaled as quite the hero for his people and it was no surprise that he was mourned like a king.

The turnout for the funeral had been immense, thousands of mourners had gathered, no expense had been spared. He had been awarded the highest of military honours and a burial befitting his rank and status. For many he had been no less than a man of great honour.

All these and other thoughts swirled around as her little boy sensing his mother's pain would reach up a little plump arm to touch her cheek. It was a sweet touch that calmed her in her moment of quiet contemplation and brought her back with a jolt to reality.

Her daughters and her older son had already retired to bed, they too had had an exhausting, traumatic day and she had to remain strong for what was coming.

Somehow, she had to muster up enormous willpower to help her children through the various stages of grief. They were vulnerable and hurting right now, all of them, and they needed her, they depended upon her. She was going to make it her life's mission to ensure that they wanted for nothing and felt doubly loved and secure.

* * *

CHAPTER 35

THE RITUAL OF THE DECEASED

She had never heard anything so absurd in her life. The next day, there was supposedly a ritual that involved relatives of both families, the deceased and the widowed party.

The widow had to be seated and the women lined up to place their offerings of clothes and money in her lap. It took considerable restraint on her part not to brush them aside and refuse to entertain such ridiculous customs. Her husband had just died and the judging expressions she saw etched on their impassive faces made her feel even more disconsolate.

In a mere few days she had been reduced to an object of sorrowful pity as everyone fixed their gaze upon her giving vent to statements like "your life is over" "she has fallen from a great height" "poor woman will spend the rest of her as a lowly widow" "what is she going to do with 4 children to raise by herself" and much more to Andromeda's horror Who were these people to decide what her life was going to be like and how dare they sit there and make harsh assumptions writing her off as if her only right to exist had been alongside her husband. She was grieving and the pain of losing her husband would be with her until the end of her days but that did not mean her life "was over" how illiterate and primeval these woman were Andromeda thought

She knew that she looked a picture of utter wretchedness, head bowed in shame as the women lined up to place bolts of unstitched cloth for her to make into clothes. As they piled up in her lap, she felt the heavy gentle thud of each piece of unstitched suit fall into her lap, followed by a reassuring hand on her head or a kiss on her cheek She cut a sad solitary figure in the centre of the courtyard terras long spent only to be replaced by a dullness and lethargy that now slithered its way through her veins.

The bevvy of chattering women surrounding her on all sides only added to her misery, heightening the need to discard everything and bolt from the proceedings. There was nothing dignified or humble about funerals here in this part of the country It was one elaborate display of exaggerated rituals with no benefits to the grieving loved ones and especially for the deceased All of this simply did not make any sense for Andromeda but she went along with it if only to show solidarity.

At one point she had watched her mother make her way through the densely packed women seated on the ground and make some offerings of money to Andromeda kissing and hugging her daughter as tears flowed freely down mother's cheek Andromeda understood that her mother would also have resented the bizarre custom but she had made an effort to blend in for fear of appearing distant and giving her in-laws more fuel to start a fire with.

She let her mind drift back to those countless moments her parents had had to tolerate many of the injustices meted out to their daughter and had never addressed them for fear of repercussions towards Andromeda but now everything had changed They no longer needed to feel afraid Andromeda vowed to herself silently She would not take any more of such treatment at their hands neither would her parents.

Coming back to the present as the last of the relatives had made their offerings someone relieved her by taking the pile of clothes to put away inside one of the storage rooms There was no way she would ever take or use any of these clothes given to her she told herself determinedly instead she would have them redistributed to the poor in the village Her body and mind seemed to be detached from herself .It seemed as if it was functioning by going through the motions. Most of the time she was not even aware of her conscious self to say she was operating on autopilot was no exaggeration.

These women were clueless, no tradition, custom, or belief could compensate for waves of grief assailing her as of this instant. She didn't want their well-intentioned offerings, she wanted her husband back, plain and simple. She knew she was being delusional, which assumedly accompanied any grieving process she thought despairingly.

* * *

CHAPTER 36

40 DAYS AND 40 NIGHTS MOURNING THE DEAD

Andromeda sat down upon the customary sheets draped across the inner courtyard floor. Chairs and sofas were rarely used in villages except indoors that were built to accommodate a few people. Sofas were considered luxury only for rooms designated to receive special guests.

Plus, it was impractical, not to mention inconvenient, to have a lot of furniture items in her village home. The dust, heat and flies were a constant menace and keeping things clean and dust free was next to impossible. Traditional hardwearing furniture that stood the ravages of village life were an all too common feature of many village homes.

She was sitting as usual on the floor quietly lost in her own thoughts as the usual gathering of villagers arrived early morning to take their seats, some new faces constantly coming and going. She hardly recognised any of them. How could she? She had never been allowed to venture outside the four walls whenever they had come over for summer and winter vacations.

Only her in-laws who had spent their entire lives here knew everyone by name. Going outside for any reason always meant covering up and observing the veil in order not to be looked at by villagers struck her as a paradox as everyone knew her in-laws but in the interests of observing a modest appearance to the villagers and exuding respectability gave them a certain kind of reverence in the eyes of the village people The rule applied to all women in the tiny village. Moving without a veil or full covering over one's dress was tantamount to committing a crime in the unspoken rule of rural life. As there was very little to do to pass the time here the villagers loved to talk and gossip everyone knew.

These women evidently formed the community and had been known for years to her mother-in-law. Her older son would spend his time with the men and guests outside who gathered in the adjoining hall outside, a segregated quarter for men only known as the "BATIQ". Most of the business and talks between village elders and themes of the house were conducted away from the women.

The veil and chador a long consisted of a long piece flowing piece of fabric that shrouded the village women. It was very rare to see women even those that worked in the fields to walk about faces and heads uncovered. There was an unspoken rule of concealment from the opposite sex that prevailed in most villages.

* * *

CHAPTER 37

SIGN DOCUMENTS

It did not take long for the true colours, if not already apparent over the years, for the brother-in-law to emerge from his short-lived den of mourning as he approached Andromeda to accompany him to the nearest district office a few miles away by motorbike to sign some documents.

Her heart was thudding rapidly, threatening to burst forth from her chest as the ringing in her ears grew louder. She could hear the faint distant din of people's voices, competing over one another. Adrenalin was coursing through her veins. Something was taking hold of her, warning her loud and clear of the imminent danger stood before her. All her senses were now fired and on high alert as her intuition kicked in. A desperation she had never seen before, showed up on her brother in laws face, as he pushed the papers he had been holding towards Andromeda.

Red flags were popping up in her head, as she met his impassive face, pinched and contorted with barely concealed hatred for her, waiting for her to take the pen and papers he now held out to his sister-in-law.

Andromeda refused to take the documents, thwarting her brother in law, which had angered him. He walked away hurriedly muttering curses under his breath as Andromeda watched him, standing her ground, aware that she had won a small victory, but the battle was far from over.

Her refusal had inflamed her in laws further, as their plan had failed so far. Thinking it was going to be a cake walk to coerce Andromeda into signing over the lands, in the midst of her grief and when she was at her most vulnerable, they had grossly misjudged her. This called for a different plan of action.

The documents in question attested to Andromeda and her children's share of the lands which were a significant portion of the estate, and would yield great dividends in years to come if managed properly.

By signing them over to her in-laws, she would be relinquishing her ownership and handing her children's inheritance to her in laws, which is what they desired. Her husband was barely cold in his grave and the wheels of greed and avarice were in full motion. They had thought she would relent without protest. They couldn't have been more wrong.

Andromeda watched in stupendous fascination the antics of these people who had professed to love him to the point they idolised him. They had cultivated many a favour from his endless stack of resources in the military and his expansive network of contacts.

They barely looked at Andromeda and her 4 fatherless children as everyone bustled about attending to the mourners. Casting a few furtive glances however in her direction told Andromeda that she was no longer welcome in this house. That was when she made her decision to return to the city and pack up her belongings. Her parents had already left and returned to the UK. They had remonstrated with their daughter, pleading and begging her to return with them.

Hostilities from Andromeda's in laws were all laid out in the open, and they knew their daughter was longer welcome amongst these cruel and vindictive people. They had no morals or an ounce of human compassion, and would go to great lengths to make their daughter's life a living hell had she stayed on.

For years they had done that but had only been restrained by her husband, only just. From day one of her marriage she had known how they had felt about her, they had never tried to disguise their scorn and hatred towards her.
Now they had only one agenda and that would be a cakewalk, they thought gleefully to themselves.

Her children were young and there was no one here on her behalf to dispute any claim or come to her defence. She was not well versed on the lay of the agricultural lands owned by her husband, as throughout their marriage he had solely attended to the day to day running and maintenance of his lands back in the village alongside his job in the city.

Andromeda was clueless when it came to such matters. In clear uncertain terms her husband had the patriarchal mindset that women were relegated to the role of housewife and parenting duties, the men tended to matters outside the home which included agriculture and husbandry. Her husband had ruled the roost with an iron fist, and Andromeda was never consulted on anything that involved business, finances or his dealings with others.

Andromeda had noted with interest that although Patriarchy was written all over in the mindsets and cultural traditions within her in laws, especially her husband who had been programmed to adhere to these norms, the Mother-in-law was the Chief matriarch behind the wheel. Nothing got past her without her approval. She was the proverbial iron fist that ruled the household.

* * *

CHAPTER 38

LINES ARE DRAWN

Now the dynamics had shifted. No one had seen this coming. He was gone, the children could not contest or fight alongside their mother for their inherent rights. They were too young and had not come of age. This made things a whole lot easier for her in-laws paving the way for them to swoop in like hungry vultures and seize her children's inheritance down to the very last dime.

Being a respectable married woman was a status upheld in society and family circles. It was a sacred union, companions for life, for better for worse, the thrill of dressing up, travelling the world, making wonderful memories and most importantly watching one's children grow up. These were all yet to be fully lived. The notions of becoming grandparents one day another, much sought after wish of most parents.

His sudden passing put paid to this and much more in one instant. All the plans they had made together and places yet to visit together and watch their children become exceptional adults one day had all been ruthlessly quashed by the unrelenting hand of fate.

The faintest or tiniest bit of respect Andromeda could have hoped for was stripped and she was met with open, cold hostility in its stead. She had tried on numerous occasions to approach her grieving mother-in-law, only to be met with a cold response that caused her to shrink back, and retreat At first she had thought her mother in law needed to have space in which to grieve for her son, for no mother or parent should ever have to outlive their child. It was not natural. Andromeda could feel her mother-in-law's pain. It was a loss that she prayed no parent had to endure in their life time. However as time passed her mother in law barely registered Andromeda's presence and had not once spoken to her since the funeral. It was odd considering that they were both grieving a huge insurmountable loss and needed to be there to support one another. Instead the lingering silence and cold treatment spoke volumes. It was as if now that her husband had gone, she was no longer a person of any value or concern to them. She was ineffectively dismissed and no-one would be sad to see her go, Andromeda thought , feeling another wave of rising helplessness and grief rip through her at such coldness from her in laws.

"Till death do us part" could never have been more true than in the realisation that it was not just her husband who had parted ways but all that was associated with him. A single tear trickled down her cheek.

According to her mother-in-law whose life had been dictated by age old customs of patriarchal tradition, Andromeda had been upended from her lofty perch and stripped of her status, her rights, her feelings, her wants and needs were no longer of any consequence.

* * *

CHAPTER 39

GREED

The sprawling agricultural lands, which belonged to her husband and his younger wayward brother spanned for miles in the district. Rich and resourceful in crops and an abundance of food year in year out, it had been her husband's pride and joy. Every year his family had reaped the bounties and fruits that the lands had provided, from the famous succulent juicy oranges of the Punjab to mouth-watering mangoes, and watermelon. They provided Andromeda's kitchen with flour and rice which and lasted the summer and winter months.

Now that the inheritance automatically transferred to her and her children, her in-laws had begun assembling in corners away from any eavesdroppers. Talking frantically in hushed groups, gesturing wildly with her arms, her mother-in-law was clearly unhappy and was trying to put a point across, sometimes jabbing at empty air to enunciate something. It was painfully obvious from their mannerisms and piercing looks directed at her, that they were planning and plotting some nefarious scheme.

Andromeda's suspicions were confirmed when her brother-in-law summoned her on the night of her husband's funeral clutching a sheaf of papers. He had told Andromeda that at first light she had to prepare to leave with him to another town at an hour's drive away where the land registry office was located.

She was required to sign some important documents. As to what the documents were he did not say, assuming his not so smart sister in law would not think twice about hesitating. In their perception she was a clueless, dim witted fool who had little to zero knowledge about land affairs. Especially the large tract of land she had just inherited following her husband's death. Unless they managed to elicit her signature signing everything over to her in-laws she and her children would be the sole owners of 50% of all agricultural land the other 50% belonging to her brother in law. Yet greed knew no bounds they wanted it all and the newly widowed Andromeda was not going to walk away with her share if they could help it.

Despite being in the throes of her grief herself, Andromeda did not need any of this right now, her priorities were her children and it was all she could do to stay alert and watch over them as any protective mother would. She still had her senses about her. Her senses right now were screaming at her that something was off, the timing was wrong, and it threw up a slew of suspicious motives which prompted her to refuse her brother-in-law's strange request. What was the urgency, why the rush, his brother had barely been in his grave less than 24 hours? Surely these things whatever they were, could wait. She had her suspicions but she kept them to herself Aside from her parents there was no-one she could trust here. Everyone around her wanted something or the other from her.

As expected she was met with a disgusted glare and reprimands from her in-laws. They had not expected Andromeda in her current state of mind to refuse any request, much less have the capacity to understand for what reason they wanted to obtain her signatures.

* * *

CHAPTER 40

THE AGENDA

The agenda was in full swing, as plans were put into motion. Andromeda's in-laws were hell bent on their course of action. They would utilise all their powers to restrict access to her now inherited lands. If that meant bribing officials, and planning corrupt ways to seize her assets under her nose, they would do it without a moment's hesitation. Land ownership was a mark of great wealth and status for the privileged few. The more acres one owned, the more elevated their position in society became.

However what had struck Andromeda with surprise, when she first arrived that was the way her in laws lived in the village. In spite of having large tracts of agricultural land and reaping the huge benefits off the yields from cultivated crops year in year out, they still lived frugally. Dried, mud and clay baked rooms made up the interior of the house, with, open air cooking on makeshift ovens hewn out of the same baked clay. The living arrangements overall were very basic and dated.

The next few days would be crucial, muted conversations, snatched glances in her direction, and only heightened Andromeda's anxiety. She was all too aware of how rapidly things had changed for her, amidst her grieving, she had to deal with all these people and their open hostility.

Soon it would be time for her parents to leave. Her parents who had flown from the UK to be by their daughter's side, Andromeda to return back home with them and her children, where she would be taken care of.

There was nothing more for her. Much to everyone's surprise and horror, Andromeda refused, explaining to her concerned parents that she had matters to settle and her late husband's affairs to conclude. She could not leave without ensuring that her children's future was secured. Although she had very little knowledge as to how she was going to manage all this by herself but one thing she was certain of, was, her in laws could not be relied upon much less trusted.

When they heard that she was staying back, and her parents would return to the UK alone, this had enraged them, and thwarted their best laid plans. This they had not expected from the meek, placid and useless Andromeda. She had lived in her husband's shadow for years and under their power. What was she going to achieve staying back?

Her mother in law, seething in frustration was not dissuaded by her daughter in law's decision. She had resolved to make life miserable for her daughter in law in the coming days.

She was still he Matriarch and the head of the family. She would make sure that any legacy left by her late son would not go to her daughter in law and her children. The sooner Andromeda could be ousted from their lives the sooner they could all move on.

* * *

CHAPTER 41

THE PAGREE RITUAL

Andromeda was talking with her aunt. They were amongst many of the close relatives who had come from other towns and cities and were staying a little longer much to the chagrin and annoyance of her in-laws. It was the culture here. There was no such thing as guests overstaying their welcome, they had carte blanche to stay as long as they liked. The hosts could do little else but grin and bear it. To do otherwise would render them ungracious.

They had all been amassed in the open courtyard conversing amongst themselves, some sprawled or sitting cross-legged on charpois. A time-honored invention which had been passed down by the ancients, and now took pride of place in many homes across the world. These woven benches also doubled as beds interwoven with colourful rope, resting atop 4 beams attached to four legs that curved intricately giving them an imperial look.

Andromeda found them to be coarse and irritating to sit on at first, the ragged rope made her want to scratch profusely. It took some getting used to. These beds had been placed around the yard. People were milling about as children laughed and chased each other around the open space squealing with delight and the adults talked amongst themselves. She spotted her little boy being led by his cousins who fussed over him, with joyful delight.

Ibrahim was not sure of friends here. They all wanted to play with them, her other children were milling about also, chatting with cousins they had hardly met and were getting acquainted. Andromeda found some comfort in her mother's relatives, the aunts and uncles who had stayed on after the funeral. Andromeda had already discovered to her shock, that they were all closely connected with her in laws by way of intermarrying amongst themselves.

The fleeting thought that she would have any allies here just as swiftly vanished.

Something was happening today, Andromeda could sense a prickly tension in the air. She found as usual her sisters-in-law and mother in law huddled in a corner talking away furiously backs hunched in unison as their hushed whispers, blotted out by the clanging pots and pans and frenzied activity all around them seemingly oblivious to all else

The meeting seemed intense Andromeda observed as now and again her sister in laws and brother in law lifted their heads to throw her a surreptitious look. What were they up to she wondered As she busied herself tending to her son who was tugging at her hem, he had grown tired of playing with his cousins and wanted to be picked up.

Hoisting her sleepy child onto one hip she carried him to the small kitchen to warm some milk for him before he fell asleep. The kitchen which comprised a single basic room with grey cement floors and plastered walls was one of the least favourable rooms in the house Dull white washed paint peeled away now looked yellowish in other places the walls looked blackened from the stain of the smoke from the gas cylinders used for cooking indoors when the weather was rainy.

Two slabs of concrete were crudely attached midway along the small grimy kitchen wall set at an angle to form an L shape to form a makeshift counter top on which a manner of utensils were sprawled carelessly in an untidy fashion, a single solitary light bulb hung dangled on a fraying wire from the ceiling.

It was still an improvement despite the lack of cupboards and some sort of organised work space. When she had first arrived the kitchen had been little more than a rustic shed with a wood and straw thatch roof and two open air clay.

She did not want her son to go to bed hungry. All semblance of routine went out of the window on occasions like these. Cooking and serving food was haphazard at best and although they had domestic help her mother in law often recruited "cooks" from outside to prepare huge hulking cauldron type of pots of bubbling meat curry and rice which was served the next day also. The meeting over her in-laws had dispersed to see to the bedding arrangements of the guests.

There were still a number of relatives who had stayed over after the funeral. Breakfast was a simplistic affair and cheap, Andromeda noted in all the years she had come to her in laws home. Steaming cups of desi Chai (milky Tea) was served with dry rusk biscuits that were dipped in the tea and consumed, because it was far more cheaper and economical to buy in bulk and serve to a large number of guests, especially on such occasions as these. No one had the time or resources to cater for flamboyant meal preparation.

Her brother-in-law had also come in from outside where the men and guests were still assembled. His mother had summoned him and spoke something in his ear. He listened to to his mother intently avidly casting surreptitious glances her way that Andromeda found disconcerting to say the least.

There were clearly up to something, what it was she nor the unsuspecting assembly of guests could fathom. If there was one thing Andromeda had learnt in 13 years of observing these people and families in her parents' circle, it was the politics, and backstabbing that was at the heart of every family, which would spill over into other families.

There was never a moment of peace and only warring factions over the most trivial and pettiest of things. There was no filter and diplomacy.

It was around midday that commotion broke out in the home. Andromeda had not paid much attention to the whispers and protests going on around here as she was barely functioning, on auto pilot just going through the motions for even now 10 days later it still felt like a bad nightmare. It all seemed surreal and she felt like she was descending deeper and deeper into a pit where only darkness lay A lethargy was creeping over her making her want to shut down little by little until she could no longer feel any semblance of reality.

She was trying to distance herself from her own reality perhaps that was what it was maybe a mode of self-preservation. Until the moment she had received the news of her husband's death, everything had ceased to make sense

The rumblings and the unmistakable sound of angry voices were growing louder, followed by more bickering. She then saw her brother-in-law walk back through the open entrance door. Following the suspicious meeting with his mother and sisters he had slipped out of the house only to re-emerge moments later with a group of men matching his defiant stride, his back bore the stiffness and poise of someone who had taken charge and knew he was the unelected leader to replace his deceased brother. He was not a tall man and short of stature with unappealing features and a sneer that lent him a sinister appearance. The determined look on his face, attempted to relay a message to all those who were staring that now he was in charge. His jutting jaw defying anyone who dared to oppose him.

As if emboldened by his family he strutted up to the house to where all the waiting relatives gathered to watch No-one knew what was coming next as nobody had been given any heads up Andromeda suspected that her in laws had something up their sleeve given the surreptitious glances they gave each other and the smug knowing expression upon her oldest sister in laws face was irrefutable proof that the next move would be an announcement of sorts a declaration of power shifting from older to the younger brother.

Though they were not rich or wealthy by any standards the mentality reflected the opposite They wanted to be seen to wield power over the village and the relatives by virtue of their land ownership according them a higher status to those who had marginally less Andromeda's mother in law was a fierce advocate for the rules of patriarchy and now it was no different from one son to the other she wanted the baton to pass to her youngest son.

Andromeda watched from her seat, open mouthed at the unfolding scene in front of her. The mother-in-law strode up to her son, mouth firmly set and brooking no interference from anybody. Without further ado she and her eldest daughter placed a piece of headgear, a pagree, atop her son's head proclaiming him the rightful heir to his brother and now proclaiming that following his brother's death, he was the sole head of the household and all rights therefore to be transferred to him.

At this all hell broke loose, chaos prevailed, everyone present were up in arms at this gross display of injustice, the ceremony itself was unwarranted at a time like this, it was a macabre almost insane display of transferring of patriarchal power to the next "man of the house" Andromeda's brother in law. The relatives shouted their protest in unison, letting their anger be felt towards Andromeda's mother in law who by this time had realized she and her daughters were grossly outnumbered and began backtracking. Their theatrics had not gone unnoticed all this while not to mention their derision and contemptuous behaviour towards Andromeda, but now to make a show of proclaiming her son as the next heir when the real heir stood a mere feet away had been enough to unleash everyone's anger. All this while Andromeda and her children had looked on in silent anguish. Her oldest child, Samuel, the true heir to his father now, watched wordlessly as the pantomime before him unfolded. Such was the anger and rebuke from the relatives that she watched her mother in law hastily remove the head gear from her son's head who now scowled at everyone. His gaze locked with Andromedas filled with hate and scorn as his mother now sheepishly instructed her son to step down from the steps leading into one of the stores of the house on which the ceremony had been about to take place, before everyone had staged an immediate halt to the proceedings. As relatives took the rise at the ridiculousness and unfairness of it, gesticulating wildly to her. Andromeda's son, who was a lanky boy of 15 years, sat by his mother's side observing the proceedings quietly, heart laden with grief, nothing was of any consequence to him. He missed his father.

The relatives had made such a hue and cry admonishing Andromeda's mother-in-law that the rightful heir in this house was now the oldest son and not his brother who had seen fit to take on the mantle without further ado. They would not simply sit back and let such blatant injustice be done. The boy, his mother and siblings were the beneficiaries and heirs and it was as pure and simple as that.

With great reluctance and mutterings the other in-laws eventually agreed but not without fixing Andromeda a stare of such malevolence that she felt herself shiver.

* * *

CHAPTER 42

RETURN TO ISLAMABAD

Time passed, sifting through affairs, probate, unresolved unfinished business of her late husband; there was a plethora of details to finalise. Above all she needed to look for a home for her and her children.

Her in-laws had deemed it fit to come and pay her a visit, the shenanigans in the village well and truly forgotten. Andromeda had welcomed them into her home for the sake of peace and respect for her deceased husband's family, but they had proved to be less than helpful and like a leopard unable to change its spots, they had come not for her and her children but to keep up a modicum of appearances to see what could be salvaged from her inherited possessions.

Andromeda had returned to the village a few times in a bid to reconnect with her in-laws. She had bought a car which made it a lot easier to travel without the hassle of unreliable public transport. However, after arriving at her husband's village home, Andromeda received not the warm welcome she had envisaged, but an icy reception instead.

She felt the unmistakeable icy chills like cold fingers from the depths of a glacier encircling her whole body, her sister-in-law stood rooted to the spot beneath the veranda circling the main portion of the house, half concealed by the shadow of the sinking rays of the sun, her eyes glaring silently across at Andromeda, who stood a few yards away with her children in the entrance of the big metal gate that led into the courtyard of their village home. No one spoke or said a word. There was another relative who Andromeda recognised to be her husband's aunt, she stepped forward to give Andromeda a hearty embrace and with a smile, welcomed them.

It was apparent more than ever to Andromeda's dismay that, any hopes of reconciling with her husband's family were dashed. It was an awkward exchange that ensued with the minutes of a clock ticking nearby sounding resolutely to fill the walls of silence that crept up between them.

They did not beckon her in, or welcome her home. It was the first time, Andromeda had ventured back to the village after her return to the city, where she had hired a truck to transport belongings from her husband's village to her new home in Islamabad. She remembered with painful sadness how they had treated her then following the funeral.

They had fought and cursed her in front of her father as she had silently made her preparations. She had put it down to their inconsolable grief and let things slide. Emotions had been running high understandably, for they too had lost a son and a brother. Things would surely get better in the days that followed as the raw grief turned to a reluctant acceptance and life resumed back to its normal pattern.

It took her a moment before realisation set in, how foolish she had been and naive to imagine that they would want anything to do with her and their brother's children. The bridges were well and truly burnt if their cold frosty reception was anything to go by. Andromeda was no longer their concern or welcome back into their fold.

It was uncanny, here she was the victim of fate of life's tragedies, suffering and worrying about the next meal, how would she feed her children, where would they live? How on earth were they going to manage, how would she pay the bills, provide for her children?

She didn't have the means or the skills to make a living for herself. Had she completed her education or used those years to train and acquire some skills at least she would have stood some semblance of chance.

Yet here she was, being punished for something which that fate had delivered to her in one sweeping unapologetic blow. Society shunned her, her own parents had their own hands full, and short of saying it out aloud, she had to manage for better or worse on her own with 4 children. A burden they were not willing to share or support her with for she and her children were indeed a burden to all those who had known her.

The same evening as dusk had set in, although it had not been safe to make the drive back to the city, which was a 3-hour drive in the night, Andromeda had decided to leave there and then. Nobody stopped her or asked her to remain, and leave in the early hours.

They remained impassive and unmoved by her decision to go. It was a further confirmation that she was an outsider in her own home, and to remain would only invite more grief and torment. It was a painstaking drive back, fear and terror wracked through her soul, as she lamented inwardly at her foolhardiness. No lone woman drove on silent treacherous roads at this time of the night, roads that would take her through forbidden zones, through dark mountain passes, and salt ranges that towered like menacing giants in the dark.

That night as she drove, silently muttering prayers all the way, her heart in her mouth, and her palms cold and clammy with terror, she gripped the wheel with ferocious determination and ploughed her way through the winding roads of Punjab, praying and pleading to God to save her from any unruly bandits and lurking predators. She was truly alone in the world now, and only God could save and protect her from whatever dangers lay ahead. The children slept fitfully in the back, oblivious to their mother's predicament. She vowed to keep them safe.

* * *

CHAPTER 43

RULE OF PATRIARCHY

One could even go as far as presuming that in patriarchal societies, such as Andromeda had endured, the widowed woman was little more than a pariah, relegated to the lower strata of society as well in the eyes of family and other relatives.

From her own bitter experience, Andromeda had run the entire gamut of feelings from guilt to sorrow, and an inane sense of injustice. It was unbelievable how people could change with such rapidity towards widows like her. Widows who had gone from being nurturers and homemakers to the lowest ranking and untouchable segment of a close minded society.

* * *

CHAPTER 44

THE ARRIVAL OF TRUCKS

The loud rumbling noise of the monstrous trucks drew close as everyone watched from the balcony stretching out across the front end of second floor flat Mouths agape they had watched with stupefied expressions the clearly marked Chinese logo of the vehicles containing the possessions which Andromeda and her husband had picked out painstakingly over 4 years of their time in China It was a pitiful reminder that sent waves of sorrow cascading though her being.

A culmination of tireless hours spent each weekend of those 4 years of collecting furniture and household items from their travels all over China. Items that were undeniably priceless and exotic, from the thick handmade Chinese silk rugs to the intricately carved rosewood furniture and a countless collection of dazzling ornaments engraved with jade and ebony and filigree etched into pieces of furniture that were stunning beyond comparison.

There were many valuable pieces that her husband had spent laborious painstaking hours searching for in the countless unending maze of markets and shopping precincts ,dotted all over the large cities and even remote villages that were a several hours drive from Beijing. It had been worth the long arduous treks, for her husband was an immensely house proud man who loved to entertain friends and important persons at home, he wanted to show off his vast collection of expensive artefacts. His home and lifestyle were his pride and joy, it was all about the appearance and impression he wished to cultivate across. Many of the things they had accumulated had been inspired by visiting the homes of diplomats and dignitaries in addition to his numerous travels across the provinces and other countries. There was never any shortage of conversation around the home as many proudly displayed decorations made for good conversation pieces.

Many luxury items had been presented as gifts from distinguished dignitaries and heads of state in recognition for his services, and when they had been invited to dinner, they came bearing gifts.

In the 4 years they had lived in china, everything they had bought together had been meticulously planned for the huge house her husband had dreamt and envisioned building one day in the foothills of the lush sprawling city back in his home country. It was as all he ever talked about.

A home to rival all the other magnificent villas and 4-storey complexes that graced the more affluent suburbs of the city His home would be replete with only the best furnishings and designed to a breathtaking standard. He could not wait to return to his country and begin the process of constructing his dream home.

They had selected dozens of 6th century style black lacquer furniture from tall folding screens with carvings of painted ladies and butterflies and flowers to coffee tables and chairs and a bed that would show off their home to perfection Andromeda could not wait to entertain her friends and show off her beautifully decorated home once it was complete she had thought dreamily to herself She could visualise how she was going to arrange her home where everything would go Every room of their new house, yet to be constructed would be a delight to behold pieces of the orient adorned throughout the rooms.

She would be the envy of all her friends, her neighbours and even her in laws, although the latter could come to resent her even more, she knew, with a pang of guilt. They would begrudge her good fortune, of that she was certain. Except now these lumbering trucks that were now grounding to a shuddering halt beneath the apartment were a painful l reminder of a dream that once had been. Any joy or excitement that had once been associated with accumulating the beautiful things together had been eviscerated. It could all be dust now for all she cared, thought Andromeda, struggling hold in her urge to scream and cry in frustrated grief at her plight Tears rolled silently down her face as she felt a stab of pain The sight of the trucks had only served to drive home the knife of despair in her heart What good were all here things now that her husband was gone, what was she to do with all this, they had lost their charm, and worth from the moment she had learnt of his death.

Everything else had simply ceased to mean anything to her. In spite of their troubled marriage and the relentless arguing and fighting she had loved him. Now she was feeling at a complete and utter loss without his secure presence by her side.

Her in laws had accompanied her back following the end of the mourning period in the village in the guise of helping her with any unpacking and arranging matters when the trucks arrived. Now they too were openly sobbing her mother in law wringing her hands in despair, commenting on the vast bulk of possessions contained in these trucks. Her son's most coveted possessions had arrived intact after an arduous journey of thousands of miles and several weeks later, but her son was gone, forever never to return.

Her heart was filled with inexplicable grief why? She had asked God countless times, why did he have to take her son who had years of life that should've been lived. He was taken too soon from her. No parent should have to bury their child she had buried three of her children over the course of the years not. Day went by when she had when she had never thought about them Why could God not have spared her son and taken her instead as she looked across at her daughter in law, busy checking the manifest of items .

Her heart filled with rage contempt and unbridled anger at the unfairness of life It took all her inner reserves of strength not to show it For now she had to suppress, as she took into account her surroundings They were no longer in the village now, where she could speak no holds barred. It was unfair that her son had to die and Andromeda was spared She must be gloating inside the cunning sly woman her sister in laws thought voicing their opinions loud enough that Andromeda could not fail to hear.

Did they have any shame at all bemoaning and complaining nonstop It incensed her to hear the liturgy of complaints but she held her tongue Did they really think she Andromeda was so shallow that having a house filled with material possessions would compensate for the loss of her husband? If that was the case then she had been given a sore deal where fate was concerned. What she would not give to have her husband back her children's father instead of meaningless artefacts. Her in-laws would never understand that

She had busied herself in directing the labourers she had managed to hire to help her with the unloading and bringing the cartons upstairs. There was no lift so the men had to haul the heavy items up two flights of stairs. She felt sorry for the labouring men they looked malnourished and emaciated It always tugged at her heart to see lines of labourers sat on sidewalks and roads every morning wherever she went in the city or the towns They were a common sight huddled in long lines with the most basic tools of their trade hoping to get passing work in order to feed their families. The daily wages of a labourer were a pittance and life was extremely hard for these men so Andromeda tried to employ them whenever she could.

It was a shame she had not been able to prepare a meal or offer them something which normally she would do, but she simply had not found the time amongst the hundreds of pressing matters that were weighing her down

She had not expected to get any help from her in laws and she had been right, for they spent most of the time holed up one of the three bedrooms with the door firmly shut. They talked in urgent whispers, of something she could easily guess, "Her".

The group now stood back idly watching in dumbfounded fascination as the huge hefty cartons and crates were brought up and placed squarely in the centre of the rooms Her in laws her mother in law her two sister in laws and their husbands her brother in law all watched without stepping forward to offer any help or support.

It was inconceivable to think their brother had acquired so much and now he would never see the light of day to enjoy them Instead she would get everything looking in

Andromeda's direction who was busy checking the last of the unloaded boxes and signing some papers they all shot her a scathing glance resentment apparent on each person's face.

Once the trucks had departed after Andromeda had given the exhausted but appreciative drivers a hefty tip she shut the door leaning back exhausted against trying to quell her rising nausea. The house was cast in darkness. Like shadowy monsters the imposing hulk of boxes sat piled in various stacks There was so many containers and crates scattered all throughout the flat What on earth was she going do now with all this lot, she had thought despairingly, panic rising in her chest It had occurred to her already that in one months' time she had to vacate this apartment and find a place along with storage where and how was she going to manage this all by herself.

Then she heard a whining plaintive cry recognising the shrill undertone of her younger sister in law.

"Why does she get to keep all this, she is a conniving greedy woman who has everything now that my brother is dead. She is going to take it take it all. We have nothing."

They had tried to shush her but it was too late Andromeda fought the urge to say something back in retort but managed to restrain herself Why were they all here if all they were going to do were to throw rejoinders at her and give her endless guilt trips At this moment the only guilt she was feeling was survivor's guilt She had welcomed them as she had done before countless times, except now she was here alone without her husband. She had promised herself that she was, going to respect and support her mother in law so that they would not have any reason to feel that she had abandoned them. Yet they were not making it easy for her at all. If anything they were driving her away by the way they were behaving towards her.

* * *

CHAPTER 45

ADJUSTMENT

The fateful day when she turned from a doting wife to a 31 year old grieving widow arrived and turned her whole life on its head. The journey as a widow had begun. Uncertainties lay ahead. Like the empty bleak vastness of a desert plain, stretching on for miles into nothingness, Andromeda saw that her life appeared barren without the comforting presence of her husband by her side.

Her mind was in overdrive as a tumult of questions raced through bombarding her senses until she felt dizzy. She did not have a clue as to how she would proceed from here on. As her widowed status came to light, Andromeda saw to her horror that there was a sudden shift in people's perceptions, their attitudes towards her, barely made any effort to conceal their distaste, even contempt and a certain malicious satisfaction at her fall from grace as they reminded her without preamble. The terrible experiences Andromeda encountered showed her what human nature was capable of, from lacking empathy to wreaking misery upon her and other women in similar situations, which she was later to discover.

Now that she was part of this unfortunate club of widowhood, Andromeda was told of countless tales and stories from the very women who had been in her unenviable position. Those who had tragically not only lost their husbands, but their whole lives not unlike hers had been upended and turned upside down, save for the few who managed to rebuild and move on after their tragic losses. The cruel treatment meted out to them especially from their in-laws, was horrific to hear. Estrangement from family, shunned by society and the struggles they underwent whilst raising children without a father was a never-ending battle that raged for years in some cases until the children had come of age and were able to support and defend their mother.

Many of these women whom Andromeda encountered during the course of her time there had befallen hard times due to neglect, lack of family support, financial hardship, and in many cases, exploitation by in-laws to seize any assets that she and her children had inherited, through cunning means, driven by greed and total apathy for the widow's plight. She was a symbol of weakness and from whom no usefulness could be derived, she was expendable.

Inhibited by a dated belief system, her movements were restricted as would be her life going forward. Her first and foremost priority was going to be her children. She had to protect them and shield them from the incoming maelstrom of attacks and cruel taunts that were imminent from family and relatives and even strangers. She would die for them if that is what it took to keep them safe from the onslaught of those who had turned their backs on her. There were predators, at every corner waiting to pounce and try their luck at exploiting a vulnerable, weak, widow who had no shield or line of defence.

Families she thought she could depend on had simply slipped unobtrusively into the dark shadows whence they came. There were those who came to offer their help and support yet behind their guise often lay a more sinister intent, to weaken Andromeda with a false sense of security until she capitulated to their demands. They tried to buy her, woo her, and placate her with offers of help, and presents to win her over. Even offers of marriage were not held back despite her proposers having wives and families, nothing deterred them from trying their luck with the newly widowed Andromeda. These blatant attempts to gain her trust had they been successful, would have been a free ticket to the UK if they played their cards right.

Over the first few years, as Andromeda settled her affairs and tried against insurmountable odds to eke out a living with her children, many dubious characters had come knocking on her door asking for her. Her first concern had to be strengthening security, to the point she had almost fortified her home with the steel bars in every window typical of most homes there to keep out intruders.

* * *

CHAPTER 46

STRANGERS

She lived amidst a pack of vultures and opportunists alike, relatives that just emerged after decades of non-contact. Suddenly she was inundated with people trying to use her as leverage for their own ambitions.

Andromeda had been aware that her life was not going to be the same ever again, and she had to adjust to this whole new shift in her status and role as a single mother. However, what she had not been prepared for was the total lack of empathy and the cold isolation that greeted her at every juncture.

Back in the familiar compound where she had lived many years amongst families of officers and sailors, who all knew one another, she saw to her horror how those same people were now total strangers to her. The families whose children she had tutored, in English forging unbreakable bonds and attachments in the community were now unravelling before her eyes. She had dined, and entertained with them and, often, the women would meet up at frequent social gatherings or gather at each other's homes.

Now that she was a widow, those same people had morphed into these unrecognisable strangers. All traces of friendliness had vanished leaving disdain and pity in their wake.

One moment ago it seemed she had been laughing and joking as they had talked on the phone for hours and made plans, extended weekend invites and now, Andromeda found with a sickening lurch in her stomach, how they went to great pains to avoid meeting her gaze. They could barely bring themselves to look her in the eye.

These people who had once been her friends, were replaced by women in whose eyes, only a look of pitiful recognition and scorned rejection shot back to her. Any trace of sympathy, understanding, and compassion was absent.

Andromeda could understand how lepers must have felt in the days when they were cursed, and banished from society. A stain on human society and perceived as even less than human beings.

She had decided from there on to slowly and eventually withdraw from society especially from the circle in which she had always lived with her husband. Andromeda was no longer welcome there. Her fall from grace could not have been made more apparent to her. She simply did not belong amongst these people. Leaving was the only option.

* * *

CHAPTER 47

CIVILIAN

The first three years following her husband's death had been horrendous. She had managed to move to another area in which she had bought a small rundown house. At least here she did not have to withstand the glare of the people amongst whom she had spent over a decade with. There would be no more contact with them, for which she was thankful. That chapter of her life was now well and truly closed.

She shut her eyes for a moment and winced as she recalled how her husband's colleagues and families had brutally cast her aside as had her in-laws The loyalties that had been apparent once proved to be short lived and they had lasted whilst he had been alive. The dull ache in her heart reminded Andromeda of the numerous hurdles she had encountered getting to where she was now.

Asking for help and assistance had been nothing short of humiliating Her widowed status brooked little compassion only a painful reminder of how far she had fallen in the estimation of society and family They looked at her differently and disparagingly, she was judged whatever she did. She had never felt so vulnerable in her life even when subjected to her in laws harsh treatment at times. This was on an entirely different scale. Knowing that she had no back up or support, she had to find her way around the city and get things done herself.

At that time in society, Andromeda had not come across many women who were self-reliant or independent on a great scale. It felt like a damning indictment of being a widow or single woman going out shopping alone and doing chores without a man Men could take advantage in many ways from hiking up prices, to inflating costs of services, seeing there was no man to bargain and rationalise with them.

Andromeda was clueless on many things and had to learn through trial and error how to navigate her way through a man's world.

She had to start afresh now in the civilian sector. Andromeda had to begin with renewed vigour at a new chapter with her children.

At this stage, Andromeda had no idea what she was going to do, but first things first, the house had to be made habitable

* * *

CHAPTER 48

SON'S MILITARY INDUCTION

Andromeda's oldest son Samuel had managed to establish a presence and a foothold in the heart of what was his late father's most revered and cherished ancestral home and village.

It had been a difficult decision for Andromeda Giving up her child to be inducted into the army meant that he would spend months and even years away from her. It broke her heart to even think about it. The decision to join the cadets had come close on the heels of her husband's funeral. Emotions and sentiments had been running high at the time. Following her husband's death Andromeda's head spun with the monumental task that lay ahead, decisions assailed her from all side. What seemed like a minute ago she had relied solely on her husband for everything and now she was left completely in charge to decide everything herself. It was a daunting prospect.

It had been a mutual decision all round but no matter what decision she would have made at the time either way there had been so many uncertainties involved At least she had some measure of comfort knowing her child was in a safe place studying and becoming a man. Now she could focus on her three children. It was not going to be easy, that much she knew for sure. There were many things she was not clued up about, considering the last 16 years of her life, she had depended completely upon her husband for almost everything. Operating alone was not something she had ever envisaged she would end up doing. She could only try and do her best and that meant she would have to take each day at a time.

Andromeda did not quite know herself how rapidly things had progressed from burying her husband to securing accommodation for her family in such a short space of time. She had to look for schools for her children once they had moved to their new home. At the time she had not been sure she would even stay in the country.

It was not ideal for a single woman to live alone without family support in Pakistan her parents told her Too many things could go wrong and did go wrong for women living by themselves Andromeda could not argue with that She had heard too many stories and watched the news which was always depressing.

Amongst the high rates of crime and robberies women and children were vulnerable targets for seedy criminals.

Eventually after scouting a few colleges for her son and looking at the options for her eldest child it was decided to register him for a place in one of the elite cadet training academies subject to passing the entrance exams. Being the eldest out of her children her son had been very close to his father and had gotten to spend a lot of time with him Understandably he was devastated and at a loss Before either of them knew it he was inducted into cadet college which served as a boarding and educational facility providing top military training for young boys. At the end of which there would be a passing out parade and the young recruits could decide if they wanted to further a career in any of the armed forces.

It had seemed the ideal solution. Although how she was going to live without her son by her side separated by distance and country even once she returned to the UK. It pained her tremendously to accept this she knew she had to be brave for her son's sake and keep him motivated lest his morale weakened also.

They took comfort from the knowledge his father would have been proud and happy to see his son follow in his footsteps take up the mantle of responsibility and go on to become a fine young officer just like his father had been. This would be a fitting way to honour his legacy they had concluded. The dye was cast. There was no turning back Finally the day arrived, they had set off for the college It was an emotional farewell as so much had happened in the last few months The pain and grief of his father still very raw Samuel put on a brave face for his mother when the time came for her to leave They had completed the signing in formalities and taken a quick tour of the campus. Andromeda hugged her son tightly fighting back tears as she waved her son goodbye.

"This was it", she told herself. Her heart felt like it was breaking she was leaving her son behind in the academy that would hopefully be the making of him but the price of separation was almost too high to bear Only time would tell she could only pray that God gave her son and herself the strength to bear the separation and to protect him always Looking ahead she too faced an uncertain future.

* * *

CHAPTER 49

LPR – YEAR LATER AFTER THE PASSING

She had one year grace period known as LPR (Leave predatory to retirement) courtesy of her late husband's employers. They allowed her to live rent free for a year until she managed to secure some form of accommodation for herself.

Dusk was approaching as she stood in the balcony of her flat gazing out across the vast expanse of the cantonment area, with its trees lining the clean well swept roads, like soldiers stood to attention. The area was one of the best and most protected boasting breathtaking views of the hills against a backdrop of verdant green lush forest. She had loved living here, surrounded by panoramic views breathing in the clean fresh air, nature surrounding her on all sides, the memorable walks she had taken with her husband on balmy evenings when the sun was at its zenith, and the beautiful crimson, pink and blue hues, lit up the skies like an ethereal display.

The beautifully maintained grounds by an army of workers ensured the display of horticulture was in its prime. She had mingled with other families whose jobs and postings had brought them here like herself. People, walked, jogged, and inhabited the numerous parks in the sprawling compound, secure in the knowledge that in this small world, away from the outside was heavily protected and afforded them priceless security.

She had loved it here, now she had returned as a lowly widow who was on a time restriction. She knew all too well the horrors and dangers of civilian life outside the secluded compound. It instilled her with a sense of dread living without security Soon enough, she would have to leave with her children and pack her belongings to start life outside these walls. Something she had never experienced in all her married years.

Due to the political turmoil's and unpredictable changes in the government, life here was difficult for the poor and the working class. Corruption was rife, power struggles, and economic challenges, meant crime and anarchy was common place. No-one was really safe unless they could afford the security which was necessary in this part of the world.

* * *

CHAPTER 50

OUTCAST

She did find them a little superficial but that was just a little inkling she felt and chose to ignore. She never did quite fit in but made every attempt to do so, if anything more to please her husband and support him by being a respected member of the community.

That entailed being polite, diplomatic, and sociable. Andromeda never had a problem making friends. She was far too trusting and would wear her heart on her sleeve. It was hard to fathom and understand that in some cultures that is not often the case, as people would speak cryptically and even more alarming behave cryptically, a language replete with mixed signals. It was not always a case of what you see is what you get. It was a continuous battle of trying to understand and be understood. Andromeda never ever fit in, if any of the events that occurred during her marriage were to go by.

She would spend hours inwardly questioning her own mind.

Was it Andromeda's inability to understand right and wrong, her logic and reasoning were flawed? Rivers of doubt mingled with torrential downpours. Negativity was a cloak that encapsulated her when faced down in long drawn out exhaustive family feuds.

A year later Andromeda was invited to the wedding of a friend's daughter. Having spent a considerable time posted abroad, the husbands were working buddies, and

Andromeda knew the family. The minute she walked in through the foyer into the spacious banquet room where the wedding was being held, as the men resplendent in their attire congregated near hallways and doors engaged in political discussions and catching up on golf news, as lady wives mingled in the main room, a telling hush befell them as Andromeda walked past acknowledging a few greetings. She felt awkward, the same thing happened. Andromeda took her seat and spoke to her friend who had accompanied her. Looking around taking in her surroundings, she noted that many of the women present would steal glances her way but not quite meet her eye. They talked amongst themselves. She felt so alone and awkward.

Andromeda felt a decisive chill almost curdling her to the bone to feel steely eyes upon her, as she looked around coming to rest on women whom she had been friends with, tutored their children when she was a freelance English teacher but now through thinly veiled contemptuous stares, no one was willing to approach or even say hello to her. She looked around nervously and tried to control her rising anxieties. Why did it seem that being a widow filled her with guilt and a sense that she was being tried by society as if she had committed a crime of sorts? No one she knew was willing to be normal much less act normal around her. Her presence merely created an air of awkwardness and when Andromeda tried to converse with her late husband's friends and their spouses, she could not help but notice, a chilly frostiness in their demeanour. Their eyes seemed to blaze right through her core, accusatory, hostile almost, and most palpably the guards were up, as the conversations were stilted and eventually led to uncomfortable silences.

Andromeda felt like she was a contagion, the big elephant in the room, of whom everyone knew of but chose not to engage with.

* * *

CHAPTER 51

THE WEDDING

The wedding was the first event Andromeda had been invited to since her return from the village. It was the daughter of one of her friends who was getting betrothed. There were many faces she recognised as she sat down meekly on a chair towards the back row with her friend.

When the food was being served, Andromeda heard someone call her name as she stood in line at the heaped-up buffet table. She was hungry and had been looking forward to the array of dishes from where the aromatic and delicious scents wafted. She was approached by a friend of her late husband's and they exchanged pleasantries as he expressed his profound sorrow at the loss of his friend. He was in the middle of his sentence proclaiming his unwavering support and help if she ever needed it, when he stopped talking as he glanced up to see his furious looking wife headed towards them wielding a plate of unfinished food as she strode up to them purposefully.

It was then that Andromeda saw with alarm, the tall formidable looking woman wore a disgusted expression as she looked at Andromeda and then at her husband, her stern countenance created an icy chill in the air. She did not bother with any greetings or niceties which came as a shock as she had once been friends with Andromeda but now here she was casting poisoned glances and dismissing Andromeda as if she was someone beneath her. Her scathing glance was full of malevolence, that it had caught Andromeda unawares who had been about to help herself to the buffet , conscious of the plate she was holding in her hand like a shield, she quickly placed it down on the table behind her, she was speechless at her friend's apparent hostile behaviour. It had not been so long ago when they had all congregated at an annual function put on by the Navy. It had been a night of jovial laughter, amusement, merry making and lots of live entertainment. Andromeda unconsciously began to back away toward her seat, fighting back the tears she knew could resurface at any moment and wanted to be spared the indignity.

Her friend grabbed her husband's arm, who by now looked visibly embarrassed and chastened, she pulled him away as they walked off. Not once did he look at Andromeda, instead, head bowed, he briskly walked off as his wife turned to cast a poisonous glance towards the visibly upset Andromeda who knew in that instant what shame and stigma being a widow was going to bring. This was only the beginning an ominous sign of things to come.

She left the reception in tears vowing never to put herself in such a position ever again. Clearly she had ruffled a few feathers by attending the wedding alone as a now single woman, a widow at that.

* * *

CHAPTER 52

THE CLOCK IS TICKING

She recalled the one time when she had sought to get additional tuition lessons or her oldest child. After only a few sessions Andromeda's son was unceremoniously stood up by his teacher after the first few sessions, the explanation being that the tutor's wife was insecure and had deep seated trust issues regarding her husband of many years. He had been a former army man, known to have a wandering eye for the ladies and had been led down the path of temptation, with a history of cheating unscrupulously on his long suffering wife. After meeting Andromeda and seeing how young and newly widowed she was, the woman was not having any of it .She thereby shut down the tuition lessons before they had even begun, and that was that.

Andromeda was quite fortunate that she could manage for some time. However, she was not about to take any undue risks given her own situation. She was aware that widows like her with no supporting family or male members had a huge target emblazoned on their backs, for opportunists and intruders, given their weak constitution.

Her life had changed drastically. It was never going to be the same again for her or her children.

She knew she had to make the most of each precious second with her children. Life was unpredictable at worst and full of surprising turns at the very least.

As time was nearing for Andromeda to leave the flat, she began the desperate search for a house where she could live and move these heaped belongings into. She had no inkling or clue what and how to go about doing anything at all. 5 weeks remained in which she had to leave whether she found a place or not. The rules were ironclad.

The sprawling acres of verdant lush green scenery with a stunning backdrop of majestic mountains that towered against the bright blue sky ringed the landscape like a necklace adorning the hilly plains of Islamabad's prestigious and well known sector. This was where she used to walk daily with her husband soaking up the fresh invigorating air and its teeming wildlife as birds broke out in melodic chirps and whistles. It was a huge encampment sprawling with nature, nestled against a verdant backdrop of mountain ranges. All species of wildlife could be found here.

Many times she had walked on these paths in the late balmy evenings with her husband, where the loud incessant screaming of jackals and hyenas rang out in symphony from the direction of the mountains.

At first it used to terrify her but gradually she became used to it. She recalled hordes of wild boars sauntering casually with their menacing tusks glistening in the moonlight. Many military couples and families who lived in the huge compound walked here and often they would pass each other, acknowledge and greet each other warmly.

It was on one of these such walks, a month after Andromeda's return from the village. She had walked her that day upon the instigation of a friend who was helping her through the grieving process encouraging Andromeda to get out more, and focus on her health which had taken a toll following her husband's death.

Andromeda spotted a couple coming from the opposite direction, heads bowed as if in deep conversation. She knew they had seen her as she recognised the man as one of her husband's closest fellow officers, he was one of a tight knit batch of mates from college whom her husband had known since his adolescent years. They had embarked on their military career paths almost simultaneously so there was a lot of history between them as there was a strong kinship.

They often attended family events and dinner parties where there were gatherings, they would always meet up with the other families and enjoy breezy evenings of entertainment and banter. Those had been the good old days thought Andromeda with a sinking feeling in her stomach, a reminder that a lot had now changed.

As the couple approached Andromeda they passed her by a hair's breadth, quickening their steps as if she was a contagion, barely acknowledging her, as she was about to greet them warmly. The coldness and aloofness apparent on their faces stopped her in her tracks.

She had never felt so out of sorts and out of reach of these once caring, friendly people who had exchanged stories and laughed and celebrated with her. Cold impassive strangers had taken their place.

It had all been superficial, the diplomacy, the smiles, jovial back slapping, jokes and gatherings where it had almost felt like one big happy family. How naive she had been, Andromeda thought dismally to herself. Here she was repeatedly confronted with the hypocrisy of the very same people she had lived amongst for years, watched their children grow up alongside her own, she had even taught English to some of those boys and girls. Being a British born woman living overseas, her English accent and mannerisms had boded well for her in the diplomatic settings and amongst her international mix of friends

They had attended social events together, and gathered frequently at each other's homes for lively conversation and brunches and entertainment. It had been a heady mix of fun filled activities and excitement, creating some of the most amazing memories she would ever have.

* * *

CHAPTER 53

REJECTION

Andromeda would encounter many instances of rejection and people letting her down that it became an all too familiar occurrence. Her safety screen was gone and she felt naked and exposed, people were simply wary and maintained a distance, whilst others tried to draw close revealing less than honourable intentions.

Andromeda felt her body tense, and the heat rise to her face, from the sneers and malicious looks she received. It was driving her insane, she felt paranoid going out to gatherings, and the few invites she received at all, were no less discomfiting. The ladies she had once congregated with now bunched together leaving her alone, standing or sitting on the side lines, cutting a lonely figure.

Tongues had begun to wag no later than a month after her husband's passing. Andromeda had noticed this at Iftar parties, marking the celebration of Ramadan, she was often the centre of gossip. The host and hostess close friends of her husband had been gracious to invite her. However it did not take long before these invitations dwindled to nothing, and the friendships petered out. After all politeness and civility had their limits.

A widow's life really sucked, Andromeda thought despairingly. The stigma that came with it had attached itself like a limpet to her. She was an outcast, an untouchable amongst her peers. She was no longer welcome to the club in which only couples were allowed exclusive membership to. Widows and divorcees presented an unspoken threat, as did any single young woman.

Chapter 54

NAIVE WOMAN

Andromeda's naivety put her at a great disadvantage. She was new to the complex language of double meanings and cunning that existed in vast supply. People were not always what they seemed. She would take everything at face value and literally, when in reality, they meant something totally different, and at times, she was an easy target for their mockery and cruel taunts. She fought every impulse not to react She would show them in time that she was not one to be dissuaded easily. They wanted to see her fail losing her husband spelt a long decline for her as far as others were concerned. She would not give them the satisfaction she promised herself.

Andromeda struggled to understand the complex dynamics of bitter family infighting and longstanding feuds that existed in many households.

Her failure to adjust in Pakistan and with her in laws had been down to the disparity in communications. Unable to understand the hidden meanings, and sly remarks aimed at her, she had found that her own straight responses were met with reproach and condemnation. These had ultimately culminated in full on conflict in which she was always the perpetrator. She shook her head in dismay as if to dislodge those disarming thoughts.

Words spoken out aloud here came with multiple connotations and meanings which were easily misconstrued, twisted, manipulated and then fed back to her husband throughout her turbulent marriage. She had never stood a chance. They were like sly foxes circling, gnashing their teeth, baring their claws and waiting for her to slip up, by even the slightest of movements. The mindset was not exclusive to her in laws, Andromeda had discovered when she returned to the city.

* * *

Chapter 55

4 WEEKS TO LEAVE

Once settled, she began the arduous painstaking process of sifting through the reams of paperwork and post death formalities of her late husband. She had wasted no time as she busied herself straight away in sorting through all the accumulated correspondence in addition to looking for schools for her children. She knew little about civilian life, much less the schools her children would have to attend. They differed vastly to the strict military schools which were renowned for their strict discipline regimen and a broad curriculum of activities. Civilian schools lacked resources and demanded costly fees for everything from uniform to text books.

The daunting task stretched before her like a lazy yawn. There was so much to do and sort in addition to looking for a house. Where did she even begin? She felt the panic rising in her chest once more. Deep breaths, she told herself, she needed to calm down.

They were so many loose ends to tie up before vacating the premises. She could feel a clock in her far off mind ticking away like a poignant reminder that she had to hurry. She only had a few months before her lease would expire. The clock was ticking.

On the ground floor of the 6th floor apartment directly below her floor lived a neighbour with his wife and children. She had visited them by way of courtesy to introduce herself. It had turned out that the leery lurid propositions of the neighbour's husband disgusted and offended Andromeda's sense of propriety, hence she chose to maintain as much distance as possible and keep a low profile in the time she would be living here.

Unfortunately, Andromeda learnt men like him did not take rejection well. It was hardly surprising that he started a vendetta to malign and tarnish her reputation by leaving no stone unturned.

Gossip was soon circulating and gaining momentum as her character came under attack.

She was nothing more than a stigmatised widow. A woman to be avoided at all costs. Andromeda had heard from other sources that her name was doing the rounds. People could be so cruel she had discovered as they blatantly attacked her character. Her reputation was being mauled and ripped to shreds. She was pained to see this but chose to remain silent.

Knowing the people who were instigating these malicious campaigns against her, she had chosen to remain quiet and maintain her composure, some semblance of tolerance and tried to preserve what was left of her shredded dignity.

Fighting these people with obviously diseased mindsets was futile. She would get nowhere trying to go on the defensive.

Uttering any form of defence was useless. These people simply were impervious to the plight of a widow. As far as Andromeda was concerned it was a social stigma, and one where widows were relegated to the dustbin of life. Respect and forbearance and support would not be forthcoming. Propositions came flooding in, over the months of hell that followed. Married men who sought out vulnerable women to stake their claim on them a woman who would in fact be nothing more than a second fiddle, and even a second wife if she did agree. Although it did not take a far stretch of the imagination to see that many women opted for the latter due to poor economic circumstances and lack of support for them it was better than living in abject poverty and raising their children alone.

Andromeda was totally adamant, this would not be her. She would not sell herself short under any circumstance. She was in mourning and tried to fight the dark negative forces that lurked beneath the surface In spite of how clear everyone had made their feelings, Andromeda had her self-respect and what shreds of dignity remained.

She felt like a colossal failure, a huge burden to bear for everyone especially her own family. She felt as if she was holed up in some dark crevasses within the innermost reaches of her mind She could not allow her thoughts to suffocate her and succumb to the negativity that swirled in her mind She had to do something, anything that would make her self-reliant and bring some dignity back in her life She could do this. One way or the other she was going to get her life back on track.

This was no time for a pity party.

* * *

CHAPTER 56

THE HOUSE

Time was running out. She was clearly out of her depth here, and very much alone, but she had to make the best of her situation such as it was. After several days of scouting properties for rent, she decided that she had far too many possessions to store in a rented home, where there was no guarantee that she would be evicted without notice.

In most private rentals the landlord could make and break rules without impunity. This lessened any sense of security that Andromeda expected for her and her children. Had she rented a property, in the short term whilst she found her feet? In the end, she had decided upon a home that looked dishevelled and in need of some work, but it was the only thing she could afford at present.

It was an oddly constructed house with several stories and rooms that were small but it was more than adequate for Andromeda. It had needed a lot of work and cosmetic touch up in places to make it pleasant and habitable, but it had been worth it. Andromeda had poured all her monies which she had received from her husband's probate settlement into reconstructing and furnishing her new home.

It had been an extraordinary challenge, recruiting trusted builders and skilled tradesmen not to mention the huge length of time it had taken. Not all the work was done to a standard to her exasperation she had to keep changing builders and fixing mistakes of the ones who came before. It was an arduous task and one that she found completely out of her depth but it had to be done There was no telling how long she would have to live here and how soon she could return to the UK but there were many things that needed to be taken care of At least her eldest child was now on his way to establishing a potential career path in the military so she could focus on her other children. The first order of the day was to secure suitable living arrangements.

She had to supervise and manage a team of workers to ensure they completed the task to her satisfaction, for left to their own devices, she found that the quality of the work was compromised, and the men were prone to lapses of carelessness and apathy.

She had managed to make a few friends along the way although many of them were living in dire situations, from refugees to renters and a few homeowners.

Life in the civilian sector proved harrowing and brought many unsavoury characters to her door. She felt unsafe and in the glare of the spotlight. There was no place she could hide and remain out of sight. The situation was untenable she thought with despair. How long could she live here out in the open, a prime target for potential, burglars, robbers, foes, and predatory men. It was an open secret that she was a single widow, a young woman at that with children living alone on the outskirts of this dynamic twin city. The area where she lived was only a stone's throw away from the diplomatic enclave with its heavily fortified embassies and consulates. However it was also a prime location for potential criminals and unsavoury gangs prowling about at night seeking out vulnerable targets.

* * *

CHAPTER 57

UNCLE

A solution eventually presented itself in the guise of a relative. It was an unexpected respite from her present woes around security.

She eventually managed to convince an elderly uncle who was struggling financially to provide for his family back home in the village. Every few weeks he would return from his squalid rented quarters in the city to visit them. Andromeda, seeing a solution that would benefit them both, invited her uncle to stay at her home from where he could commute to his work a few miles away. He was a painter by trade, so jobs were plentiful in the neighbouring twin city. Providing him with rent free accommodation in comfortable surroundings and food in exchange for a male presence at her home would serve to detract many a wandering rogue and potential admirer.

She had spurned the advances of many unsavoury men. They were like hungry vultures circling overhead, waiting to go in for the kill. She was naive, the carrion, the bait it seemed like and in a country where unless you were fortunate to have a husband by your side or happened to be significantly well off to afford an entourage of guards or even a close knit family with protective brothers and cousins for deterrence then you were easy pickings as lowly vulnerable women.

The vultures from all walks of life circled ominously above her head. People, that Andromeda and her husband had socialised with over the years. The colleagues once who had once accorded her a position of respect and held her in high self-esteem, treating her with the reverence that one treats a colleague's wife had no qualms about letting their dishonourable intentions, be known. Especially now that there was no one to defend her against their lurid advances.

Her children were young and innocent, and here she was in a country that was as strange to her as the people who inhabited it. There was no help forthcoming from her relatives, everyone had mysteriously made themselves unavailable to her.

As time passed Andromeda realised she needed to keep her guard up and never let her defences down. She was all by herself now and there was nobody she could trust.
Familial pressures, and conservative attitudes, played a huge part in the way these women lived out their lives. Once married, they no longer had an identity of their own and were consigned instead to a life of drudgery, and obedience to the spouse's family.

Where there were children involved, then the widowed woman had to accept that from that moment on, her life was to be devoted entirely to her children Any personal desires she harboured or wished for had to be severed and quashed Widowers on the other hand, were met with more sympathy and understanding. It was not considered unusual or disapproving by society that he resettle.

It was not uncommon to find that greed, emotional manipulation by family members had no misgivings about exploiting their vulnerable status. Most of these widows became unwitting pawns for the undesirable gains of family members and not excluded to strangers who found them easy pickings.

This led many to stake out their pitiful existence in utter abject misery and total dependency on others. Those left with nothing but paltry means found themselves having to rely upon the support and compassion of strangers unless they were fortunate to have a family support system. The widow was relegated to being a charitable case.

Over the years Andromeda's role as a military wife meant that she met with countless families. Given the demands of the job, movement from base to base and locations from place to place was all part of her husband's job.

Andromeda was known by many because of the fact that she was a British National who come to the country and settled here after her marriage. It had been a huge culture shock for her and had taken a while getting acclimatised too. The heat here was so unbearable and she found the weather oppressive and stifling, but she had somehow managed to adapt. She had little choice.

Her youth and naivety, was all too apparent to everyone who met her, yet fetching. Some commented on her youth that she was a child bride. Andromeda was inexperienced at life, and still possessed a childlike immaturity that was reflected in the way she engaged with others. There were a few, Andromeda had no problems interacting and trying to fit in.

Some were drawn to her naivety and vulnerable looks. Andromeda had nothing of the sly, shrewd, and sharp wit of many of the people she encountered in this country, especially many of her relatives, most of whom she had never met. The nuances, and countless ways in which conversations were relayed was mind boggling and confusing.

More often than not conversations were misconstrued, lost in translation and this had caused many a fall out. No one was in the least bit interested and she ended up being taken to task over something she said but did not mean and the pattern repeated itself until her own nerves began to unravel from within. Her naivety and ignorance were shunned aside. Whenever she ventured forth to present an opinion, it was effectively ignored or mocked causing her to withdraw into herself out of shame. What an exhausting way to live, she thought letting out and exasperated sigh.

* * *

CHAPTER 58

MORAL COMPASS

People could be so cruel and vicious women were their own worst enemy, especially towards their own sex. Andromeda was baffled at their behaviour. It had taken several incidents in which she had encountered hostility at the hands of other women, most of whom she had known for years. The painful realization that women could be so cruel and vicious towards their own sex had made her even more conscious of her widowed status. She could not expect any sympathy or compassion from her kind.

She would go back to the UK and start afresh from there. The folk here were immune to change, especially her in-laws and most of her relatives. The longer she stayed here, the more likelihood of falling into their orthodox ways and becoming nothing more than a shadow. She was not so concerned for herself but her children deserved much better. She vowed to give them a life much better than her own, a life in which their dreams could be realised, a life in which they would, grow, and flourish, and have the opportunity to achieve whatever their hearts desired.

Andromeda herself had not been permitted to finish her education. Her parents and her husband had firmly beaten down her attempts to continue further studies favouring marriage love their daughter's academic future. She had been overwhelmed and grossly unprepared for the life that followed her marriage.

As fate dealt her a further blow, making her a widow, she was left with nothing to fall back on. The stark realisation of having little to no education, hit her like a punch to the gut, winding her and leaving her gasping for air.

How would she be expected to carve out any hope of earning a livelihood for her family? She had no education, no skills, no understanding, and no real time experience of life outside marriage.

Only she could understand with ferocity, the importance of providing a better life in which her children would be more than suitably equipped to handle themselves in any situation. She would not allow them to suffer if she could help it.

From this moment on this was going to be her priority She would do all she could to ensure, they would be raised as, strong independent, educated individuals, with skills that would see them through life.

There would have to be some compromises here and there, especially in terms of cultural beliefs. Especially, those that she had been brought up with. Times were changing and people changed accordingly to adapt and keep up She knew there would be much criticism and disapproval, at her less than stringent method of parenting, but she could not allow the displeasure and self-acclaimed judges in society who would stop at nothing dissuade her.

Their moral compass was different to hers and Andromeda stood to face a lot of backlash she knew going forward using knowledge and personal development she wanted to arm her children with the necessary tools to survive in today's world. Tools she could have benefitted from in her younger years which would have helped her tremendously today Being prepared for the unforeseen in a world where anything could happen was one of the most fundamental gifts she could try and give her children she thought.

Nothing could be taken for granted. Andromeda had learned in the most painful and traumatic way as possible, that life was unpredictable.

Her daughters especially, regardless, of religion, creed, and cultural background Andromeda wanted these attributes instilled in her daughter's from an early age. It would always be their security blanket, and she would rest easy in her own mind. In her drastically altered world, there would be no room for patriarchy, or submission. To her with both daughters and sons were equal. She had had enough Patriarchy instilled upon her to last a lifetime Modern times called for modern measures and this meant giving woman an equal standing in both the home the family and in society. Being the heart and centre of family life why could she not be accorded with similar status to the man and have as many equal rights and opportunities than men. It simply did not make any sense to her Andromeda thought. As history showed the achievements of countless women bore testimony to their sex. Not to mention there had been great leaping strides in development across the world to present day.

The emancipation of women had been gaining steady notoriety over the years Andromeda saw to her joy as she devoured the news and read books and biographies of famous women who had broken the glass ceiling and marched forward to emblazon their successes upon the minds of human kind
The very least Andromeda could do was ensure that her children had something to fall back on in the event of any unforeseen hardship.

* * *

CHAPTER 59

SINGLE MOM

The years had gone by and amidst many hurdles and obstacles strewn in her path, Andromeda had somehow managed to get her children from the toddler phase through their adolescent years and finally onto adulthood. The latter being that moment when they were sorely responsible for their own decisions and actions. Like herself they had to deal with the consequences that resulted and take accountability for them. This was real life and it was not meant to be easy that she could firmly attest to. The only way to deal with it was to take life head on and build a resistance to weakness and self-doubt. It was ok to fail as long as one did not give up. As her father had told her taking his favourite line from a book he had read "You can if you think you can"

For her children she would only be there to offer advice and counsel and venture forth if needed. As long as her adult children knew she loved them and would support them in times when they needed her. She would always make herself available for them and they knew that. Extraordinary challenges lay ahead on the journey of life but she could only do her utmost to make it as manageable as she could

She could now allow herself a slight luxury to sit back and watch her children embark on their own individual journeys, from here onwards.

* * *

CHAPTER 60

RETURN TO THE UK

Life goes on, 2006...

Each dawn brought its own share of challenges for the day ahead. She was getting there, slowly, not as quick she would have liked, but nevertheless, she was making progress, even if it was not all too apparent at first.

The co-dependency that she had on her spouse was almost galling. She had many questions and was a curious and keen learner. However, her place and duty was confined to the home only. There was no opportunity to learn about the intricacies and other skills of life outside of the home. Her husband had assumed all the responsibility in addition to managing his career he had been a proud home owner and took many things under his wing without the need to consult his wife

Andromeda had noted that the rigid strand of patriarchy ran deep in his family as it wove its unyielding thread through her home. He lived as a man as that which befitted his status both in society and in his home.

It was always the male who was inarguably the superior of the two sexes. Equality was unheard of in her family, where patriarchy flowed through the generations. Women in Andromeda's position were not expected to question, complain or have any dealings with their spouse's dealings outside the home. Everything was taken care of and nothing left for the woman to manage other than birthing and raising her children and managing a household.

Patriarchal societies and the dominance of the male meant women held very little sway in the marriage.

At that time, Andromeda had come to learn that primeval mindsets were firmly entrenched in certain pockets of society, especially within the more deprived and rural areas. Notably this was more common in villages and backward areas. The more undeveloped they were, the higher the rate of illiteracy.

Widows were considered a bad omen, ostracised by their relatives and communities. Many were deprived and stripped of their rights to remarry and inherit property, and found themselves victims subject to exploitation.

The disapproval, the arguments, the cold shoulder treatment and the isolation which was opening up the chasm each day was already deeply ingrained in Andromeda's wary mind.

In spite of religious doctrines preaching about the virtuosity of widows and how they should be treated with respect and dignity, reality was markedly different for them, as many unfortunate women found themselves thrown out by their dispassionate in-laws, ending up on the street or back into the homes of their parents for whom they became a huge burden to bear.

Andromeda could count herself among the lucky few as she at least as a British National as were her children, and therefore she could return immediately to her country and begin her life again, in better surroundings.

Andromeda possessed the steely will and dogged determination which were her constant companions during the difficult days that followed. If she was waiting for someone to extend a hand of support, she was in for a very long wait. As much as it incensed and riled her in-laws no end, Andromeda's newfound sense of independence took hold.

They had hoped to see her flounder helplessly in the gutter, and wither away in the garbs of widowhood, beholden to others and a shadow of herself. For them Andromeda's fall from grace to widowhood spelt the end of her life as her mother-in-law had succinctly put across to her especially in the company of visitors to the village home.

Andromeda had to comply and submit to her befallen fate and grow old alone, miserable and cast out from the crowd. The same adoring crowds of people, family and friends who had jubilantly welcomed her in their lives, now looked down upon her with ill-disguised pity and sadness.

One of the unsurprising ironies Andromeda experienced was the few relatives who had approached her for money and financial assistance. She was struggling to make ends meet herself, yet this did not deter the steady line of relatives who flocked to her door, hoping to snag something from her late husband's bequest.

Eventually the days began to ease out as she adjusted to life outside the compound. She was among strangers here but she learnt her way around and made a few friends in the neighbourhood. It was homely and she was able to make her presence felt.

She summoned every ounce of her inner strength to push forward and rebuild a life with her children. Becoming another widow stereotype was not an option she cared to entertain She had to rise above this if she wanted to change her situation and do whatever it took to ensure a good life and a future for her children. The manner in which people, and those confidantes who had once been close to her including all her friends, family acquaintances, all seemed to melt away. Those who lingered kept a telling distance from her as if she was a leper. Afraid to catch something from her if she came too close

The stigma of her newly acquired status deterred people getting close and somehow in their eyes she was simply a "nobody". Everything including her own identity, her status and role had been integrated with that alongside her husband's. Now he was here no longer and thus she also ceased to exist as far as anyone else was concerned.

Some of the men who had served alongside her husband, with respectable and honourable standing in the community, lived up to the age old cliché of shedding their hides to reveal, their innermost wolves in sheep's clothing. She had been approached numerous times, and propositioned, refusing each time. She had greater concerns and her only priority were her children, nothing else was possible, of that she was fiercely determined.

The months passed by in a haze of activities, all the while she sought to make decisions and find some stability for her children. The future was unknown, she had no idea what she was going to do, but for now securing accommodation and shelter for her children was a priority.

To her horror and chagrin, whilst she fought the battle to survive in widowhood, she met with some unruly obstacles

There were people who once upon learning that she was a widow tried to befriend her in the hope that she may have money and could be taken advantage of in her vulnerable state. Strangers accosted her at every turn for she had to leave the house to do her errands. This meant coming into contact with men in the bank, in the shops to finding mechanics to sorting her car out and many such incidences. Before it had been her husband who had dealt with everything himself.

She had to undertake the painstaking process of searching for schools in the area. Asking for advice, cost her the unreciprocated advances of her husband's friends and the scornful disdain of their wives. She shivered involuntarily feeling revulsion as she recalled the not so subtle remarks of the men had once worked alongside her husband began a smear campaign against. Andromeda for no good reason other than a few disgruntled men of repute whose attempts she had thwarted time and time again. This had served to embolden them further. Encouraged by her silence and her vulnerability to defend herself the spreading of malicious lies continued gaining momentum at each turn and spiralling until they took on a life of their own. Every conceivable attempt was made to try and besmirch her reputation. They were succeeding because Andromeda had no- one in her quarter to help defend her against the untruths and the lies. She could put up a feeble fight but it was futile. It was all of them an army of men and their families against one of her. She never stood a chance at the invariable odds stacked against her.

With no husband or father figure she was defenceless and helpless. Her children were not old enough and she worried about them hearing all this adding to their grief of losing their father. She did her best to protect them from the taunts and jeers of people who had now developed a sense of immoral righteousness.

She had become a prime target for their vitriolic tirades undoubtedly egged on by their wives who now seemed to see the once sweet innocent Andromeda as merely a woman with dishonourable traits a woman of ill repute. All manner of accusations, mudslinging and dishonourable attentions were flung in her direction.

Widows were not immune or sheltered from such prejudice it seemed, she was an open and easy target. Not only that but she also saw how her relationships and loyalties were tested sorely in that all-encompassing period of grief, when her world was turned upside down and she was plunged into a world of which she knew next to nothing. Try as hard as she might only darkness seemed to beckon to her an uncertain path lay ahead her journey was beginning without her husband next her.

Could she do it? She wondered out aloud? Tears pricking at the corner of her eyes.

It was going to be a long haul process she knew especially in Pakistan nothing was straightforward when it came to officialdom, and administrative matters bureaucracy was a minefield to negotiate. There were too many obstacles and Andromeda found herself chasing her tail as she traipsed through all kinds of offices and tried to seek to people who could possibly help her.

There was still so many unresolved matters that needed her immediate attention. Probate was going to prove a herculean challenge, here there was no will in place. She had to rely on the good will and trust of people connected to the legal processing the courts in Pakistan to help her. There was not a single soul whom she could ask to guide her particularly in the legal sector.

If there was one thing she had learnt being alone as a single parent people had no qualms to charge her extortionate rates no matter what office she turned to and whatever services she needed to complete her paperwork Everyone exacted a price of their own Her husband had dealt with everything in such a superfluous manner that he had gained some standing and a degree of respect wherever he went He knew how to bargain a vendor down to the absolute lowest and walk away with a profit at the same time appeasing the seller with his brusque charm and pleasant manners.

* * *

CHAPTER 61

VOID

The huge void left by a parent meant that Andromeda could not do much to help them overcome their loss try as she might, but only time would heal the wound if at all. She could only love and try to do right by them but growing up without a father was a devastating blow to each one of her children. Not a day passed when they did not remember him. He had left them far too soon. There were plans to be made and memories to construct he had talked of high hopes of seeing his children flourish and marry and make him a grandparent All this and a lot more and yet here they all were grieving his sudden loss. The world would never be the same again without his formidable presence.

From the moment they had arrived back in the UK, Andromeda busied herself the looming task at hand. Ensuring a roof over their head was her first priority followed by education which meant applying to the schools in their area, praying that there were places available. She had to look at getting a job immediately in order to feed and clothe her children. She knew it was not going to be easy given that she had an incomplete education and had never worked before

Andromeda knew the children missed their father terribly and watched them struggle on a daily basis She wanted to take them into her arms and reassure them, shower them with an abundance of love and protect them always but she knew despite her love she would never be able to lessen the pain nor fill the void left by her children's father.

Thinking back Andromeda realised that bereavement counselling would have helped her and her children to cope with life going forward without their father If the problems she had encountered with her youngest child had been anything to go by perhaps some form of counselling in the early days of their arrival may have benefitted him a great deal. Although he had been very young at the time his problems had arisen from primary school and continued to gain momentum. Andromeda berated herself inwardly at her lack of foresight had she known about such things as bereavement counselling she would have asked for all her children to receive it Maybe just maybe they could have managed to cope with life better

So many what ifs she pondered sighing dejectedly at the missed opportunity Maybe it was still not too late for therapy could be had at any time. She had approached the subject once or twice but her son refused flatly to entertain such a notion.

* * *

CHAPTER 62

PROBATE

Once she had settled her late husband's affairs, she had returned to the UK a broken young woman with her children, to begin to reassemble her shattered life once more.

There had not been any sort of will or adequate provision put in place for such an eventuality. Although everyone knew that death was a guaranteed fact of life No one knew when it would come but it was certain that it would come to us all eventually.

Andromeda's husband always been geared towards his career ambitious to a fault he worried and strived to the hilt towards promotions Networking for lucrative opportunities was a skill he possessed like no other He was so proficient at it that almost all his contacts had become firm friends and allies in his endeavours

Andromeda observed curiously and with avid admiration the thread of ambition woven by her husband all throughout their marriage. He seemed to be obsessed with entrepreneurial projects and aside from his glistening career she noted he would look for schemes that paid handsome dividends He was a man of many talents even though not all his quick money making schemes went to plan

Andromeda knew very little about her late husband's external activities and even less about the man she had married as she would come to know years later.

It would take years to settle her husband's affairs fully as a lot of their inheritance was tied up in pockets of agricultural land sprinkled around in the Punjab. This meant that Andromeda had very little money with which to rebuild her life all over.

There were many mitigating factors that led to repossession of her home and almost becoming homelessness and becoming destitute had fate not intervened yet again.

For one she was very naive in the ways of the world, and had made some poor financial decisions following his. After contesting and fighting numerous pleas and court appearances to transfer what little her husband had, ultimately that money too was soon gone. Andromeda never had any responsibility or handling of finances other than taking care of the home and their children.

He was borne of proud patriarchal stock predated to a time when women and equality were mere inconveniences, a non-entity as far as he was concerned. He was not obliged to share and involve Andromeda in his dealings outside the home and even in the extended family. Bringing home a pay check, paying the bills himself and giving Andromeda only enough for running the kitchen side of things, she was completely ignorant in all and everything he did.

Once or twice she had dared to question and assert her rights to be involved about her husband's handling of all financial and home related issues. This irked him and irritations ensued so eventually with a sigh of resignation, Andromeda let the matter slide sighing despondently, and wishing that her husband trusted her enough to confide in her as most married couples did. It was the norm in marriages, or so she thought. They hardly spoke much about normal things let alone matters concerning her husband's assets. It pained her because she knew this was not normal, the chasm between them was like a huge glaring monstrous mouth, that stretched imperceptibly in front of them like a wide steep ravine with no means of crossing to the other side. The only certainty was a steep plummeting death if anyone tried crossing the treacherous path lying before them. It would be a folly to even try.

He was not the person she had initially thought at the start of their nuptials, a pleasant , easy going ,charm that was difficult to avoid being unaffected by. The change had happened almost too soon in their marriage. They had grown apart. As immensely popular her husband was outside the home and in his family, with an extensive network of connections which he prided himself on, the further they had drifted apart as a husband and wife. She tried to shrug away the easy thoughts that infiltrated her mind, the helplessness and lack of self-esteem trying to worm its way through her conscience.

She felt inadequate when it came to supporting her husband because most of the time he shut her out from everything concerning his affairs and troubles. It was difficult to be the supportive wife when most of the time he never discussed his concerns with her. Her role was simply put, a wife, a mother, a housekeeper and a dutiful obedient daughter and sister in law. For the rest she did not need to know anything involving her husband's work and what went on outside.

Neither of them thought that death an inevitability would come knocking and thus turn the lives of her family upside down. Had she been wise maybe she could have prepared better for such an eventuality, by being reticent and getting to know her husband's dealings relating to their home and lands. It would have saved years of relentless hassle, and struggle, in addition to avoiding mistakes made only because she had had to guess and employ people to help her sift through the mountains of red tape and paper work.

This was why wills were made and documented so that surviving family members would face little to no opposition from various relatives looking to exploit and divulge people in her situation of what assets they inherited. The painful truth was that her husband had almost always discussed things with his family, his parents on matters relating to his estate, but she was effectively kept at a distance from such talks, perhaps they had thought her of as incapable of understanding or discussing such matters with. Maybe it was because she was a naive young woman who had lived for the most part in the UK and knew next to nothing about affairs of the land. Whatever the reason she would have listened and learned the ropes so that she was up to speed and fully prepared.

Upon her husband's sudden untimely death, Andromeda had found herself floundering in a torrential storm of uncertainty, and matters relating to her husband left her feeling in the dark for answers, clarity, and the unbending search for truth. Like a blind woman navigating the dark corridors in a quest to find answers and uncover facts, she stumbled, and fell, and had to grasp at whatever she could muster up, with no help or guidance from her in laws, who were all too happy to watch her fail in her relentless pursuit of getting justice for her children but she knew with a sinking gut wrenching feeling that she would have to fight to get what was her and her children's right. Her in laws were not about to yield and pave the way for her to reach her goal. They were and always had been heavy invested in their own agendas from the very start. It was a shame that her husband had not been able to fathom that, blinded by his unwavering sense of loyalty and responsibility to his kin, he had effectually ignored their red flags, and warnings to the detriment of his own wife and children. Now he was no longer here to see for himself and stop his family in their tracks, they worked with impunity at destroying Andromeda ensuring that she would leave with her children with nothing if their best laid plans came to rest.

* * *

CHAPTER 63

THE SON WHO STAYED BEHIND

Even months later after they had arrived back to England Andromeda's heart ached for the son she had left behind. She had settled her husband's affairs after what seemed like an interminable period of stress fighting her way through the system that was male dominated and unforgiving especially for lone females as herself. She had been left with no choice but to sell her home and leave the country. Her vulnerability as a widow and a single mother had left her exposed to the many unruly characters that were making her life miserable. Continuously propositioned and approached by strangers and the men who had once been her husband's work colleagues made her feel ill at ease.

It had been a discomfiting experience to communicate with the opposite sex, wherever she went Women she discovered were little more than sexual objects regardless of their station in life married or not unless they travelled with a male chaperone they would always be subject to some form of harassment and unwarranted intentions from other men.

Andromeda had little issues with the culture itself but more with the rigid mindset of her expanded family of relations and in laws Over time she had become a complacent victim trapped in a judgemental society in which every move, every action each word she uttered had been closely scrutinised Misplaced guilt followed her everywhere sticking to her like an unwanted shadow as did the roving pairs of eyes detailing her every movement, shadows that moved in the night.

She could feel the trees whisper to themselves as she drew close.

Her senses were heightened to the point she almost felt paranoia creeping in. There were people she had known for years who had become suddenly averse to meeting her. The guilt Andromeda felt was not of her own making but the reaction of others induced her to think she had done something wrong and she was to blame for her pitiful circumstances.

She had never so felt alienated and an outcast amongst her own people. It had been the right decision to leave, she thought. There was no life or future for her and her children. Her son who was in the cadets would one day come back to her, she would suffer the pangs of loneliness every single day, being separated from her first born.

She was stuck between a rock and a hard place, but hoped and prayed that their situation would change for the better and her whole family could. It was no longer safe for her as widowed woman to reside here alone with young children!
He was her pride and joy her first born, she loved him beyond anything she could describe, more than life itself, yet destiny had taken him away to another country in which he sought to follow in his father's footsteps and continue on his legacy.

It was the making of him, a fine young soldier had emerged through her sacrifice of sending him away from her. He had evolved as a brilliant young man, of whom she could not have been more proud.

* * *

CHAPTER 64

UK FAMILY

In the UK, life was no less easy. She had returned to her roots. Years of marriage had hardened her and political tensions and conflicts between her in laws and her parents had put a considerable strain on her relations with her own family.

Nobody had escaped unscathed from the continued backlash that had emanated from her in-laws towards her parents.

The ties had long been fractured and nothing was ever the same again. Everyone busied themselves in their own individual lives. Andromeda's siblings were embroiled in their own myriad of problems that daily life brought Her parents had aged considerably from the moment the devastating news of their son in law's death had hit them they were now faced with the additional worries and concerns for their widowed daughter and her four young children She was still very young and to have to bear such a huge tragedy at this stage and left to fend for her children alone had all but destroyed her parents.

Andromeda's parents knew that their daughter's in laws would be loath to step-in and take care of her, given their bullying actions in the past towards their daughter. They were struggling themselves to make ends meet and as painful as it was to admit it they simply could not take on the additional burden of their widowed daughter and her children She had to do it herself They would help her and support her wherever they could but it was an unfortunate tragedy that had befallen their daughter and now she would have to bear the burden alone It broke her parent's heart They had never felt so helpless as they did now.

Tensions, flared in the parental home, Andromeda was struggling, her children were bewildered confused but they needed stability and right now it seemed as she was the only one who was going to have to do it.

Her siblings over time had become strangers to her. Through no fault of her own, for she had been a victim of circumstance and the ill-fated decisions imposed by her elders on her from the moment she had finished school. Her marriage to a distant cousin on distant shores in a foreign country that was her parent's homeland but very much alien to Andromeda had effectively created a chasm between herself and her family. They were as preoccupied with their own personal battles and endless turmoils in their own lives to take stock of their eldest sister. As a result the years had passed in a blurry haze. With its merciless speed, time flew by taking with it, lost opportunities.

Memories that had not been created, words that had remained unuttered, affections never given or reciprocated. It had all been lost to senseless whims of ego, wounded pride, and deeply entrenched grievances that refused to let go of the past.

Like her kin with whom contact was fractured at best and not forthcoming for years, Andromeda had learnt to adapt and live with the greatest sorrow of being cast aside like a useless creature of no worth and one only to be pitied and ignored. For those were the feelings that coursed through her. At every juncture and door she turned to, she was met with swift disapproval and reprimand.

Andromeda had left the UK with her father as an excited young girl who had started college and looked forward to her life as a student, yet she had returned as a married young woman and an expectant mother to her first child within the first few months. Over the years and having produced 4 beautiful children, she suffered the sudden loss of her husband in her early 30s and returned once more to the UK but this time as a widow.

She was received with the pitiful stares and sympathetic words from many people, and then silence. A complete nonchalant attitude and the palpable sense of distance manifested itself with her siblings. It was deja-vu all over.

The memories of those difficult days seemed as raw as yesterday to Andromeda. She recalled with a grimace the abject despair she had felt all alone. For nothing could be worse than loneliness and a sense of being abandoned by one's loved ones.

She felt like a frail bird lying by the wayside, too weak to fly, with its tiny heart beating erratically in its chest, yet still able to summon some inner strength to hang on tenaciously to the fragile strings of life. She had to get up, and go on if only for the sake of her fatherless children. They had no one in the world but her now, and she simply could not fail them. With this in mind, she composed herself. What lay ahead was a long lonely path riddled with obstacles and ambushed decisions that would cause her to go off charter.

The years passed with much stress, angst and brutal life changing events, yet they carried her and her children tainted by everything life threw at them. Her fortitude and patience managed to hold up in the direst of situations but she had shed more than her fair share of tears and grief.

Her family were smitten with problems of their own. Her parents had struggled and toiled endlessly through the years. Andromeda's marriage at an early age had taken her away from her family for 16 years. When she did eventually return, a lot had happened and changed. For a start she had not returned as a married mother on a visit to see them. She had come back widowed and with her orphaned children. She was as much a stranger to everyone as they were to her.

They were as preoccupied with their own personal battles and endless turmoils in their own lives. Mother was battling several health issues, Father was as per himself running around and working whatever jobs came his way. Although he was getting frailer and weaker by the day, he refused to sit still.

Andromeda had learnt to adapt and live with the greatest sorrow of being cast aside like a useless, creature of no worth and one only to be pitied and ignored. For those were the feelings that coursed through her at every juncture and door she turned to. She was met with swift disapproval and reprimand.

* * *

CHAPTER 65

HOUSE HUNTING

After a few unsuccessful moves from house to house some that were infested with rats to others that were mould infested and riddled with damp they moved into a home where she had managed to get a mortgage. The savings she had brought back with her after finalising her husband's affairs had been sufficient for the hefty deposit and a few monthly payments. She had hoped that soon she would be working and therefore in a position to continue keeping on top of her mortgage.

The few part time jobs she had secured were clearly not enough given the expenses she had of raising a family on top The children came with never ending demands of their own Just as she had feared everything came crashing down in one final curtain call. Her expenses had far exceeded her income until she had fallen behind in her payments. There was nobody who could bail her out from this.

Eventually it had got to the point she could simply had no money left to pay the hefty instalments. The savings had dried up. The bank was now on her tail demanding she pay the arrears or face repossession. A word that sent shudders down her spine.

* * *

CHAPTER 66

EVICTION NOTICE

The day was almost here She had been dreading it since it all began. The feelings of fear and horror threatened to engulf her. She was about to become homeless and destitute with 3 children, one of whom was severely autistic.

Her mother and her siblings although they lived in the same town had a lot going on in their own lives, she could not possibly ask or expect them to help her. She was in utter despair and lost. What was she going to do? How were they going to live? She could feel the walls of desperation closing in on her from all sides.

The date was fast approaching, Andromeda had been served an eviction notice by the bank. Her home was to be repossessed and eviction proceedings would ensue with immediate effect. Andromeda watched with sadness as her children whom she had fought to protect were about to become homeless She had let them down. There seemed to be nothing that she could do to prevent the rug of stability being snatched from beneath their innocent bodies.

It had all happened too fast, she was barely able to catch her breath. The momentum of events was like a fast flowing river whose raging currents were sweeping her to her ultimate doom, while all she could do was to stand by helplessly and watch her own demise.

She was very naive in the way of the world, and had made some poor financial decisions following her husband's death. This had all taken place in Pakistan where she had been the victim of several scams. Even those she trusted had betrayed her till the end. After contesting and fighting numerous pleas and court appearances to transfer what little her husband had, she had used that to live on for some time until she could secure herself a job. Ultimately, the money was soon gone. Andromeda had to think quickly on her feet what to do next.

Now that she had returned to the UK there was only one thing for it, in order to make ends meet she needed to get herself to the job centre as soon as possible and begin looking for jobs. Feeling completely overwhelmed and daunted by the prospect Andromeda realised that she had never worked a day in her life or bore the responsibility of handling the finances other than taking care of their home and the children.

* * *

CHAPTER 67

BACK TO SCHOOL

Andromeda had her work cut out as she balanced her life, with education, work, raising a family and running a house. Economically things were not looking good. She had to better her prospects somehow before she could secure a decent job. Having no skills would be an impediment she had discovered to her dismay and would put her further out of reach of any employers.

Eventually she managed to find some courses which she promptly signed upper and registered her interest. She began attending night classes. At the same time she had signed on for an online degree course. Here she had been fortunate to get some additional fee support. Otherwise it would have been impossible to do the study given her meagre financial resources.

The course was exceptionally hard, given that Andromeda had not studied since High School. Getting to grips with the academics and the highfalutin language of her subjects was virtually impossible. Not to mention the huge work load which was staggering. She had to plough her way through it, if she and her children hoped to survive the poverty that was staring them in the face.

Those 8 years had been long and by day she looked to her children, by night she spent copious hours locked up in her study poring over reams and reams of information that she had to dissect, disseminate and complete assessments based upon her understanding. To say it was difficult was a gross understatement.

Raising a family while trying to study for a degree proved to be an uphill struggle. Many times, she faltered, slipped, and had to pick herself up to continue. No one could envision the future but at least she wanted to be prepared in case of extreme circumstances where at least qualifications and a recognised degree would be able to stand her in good stead.

Her children were her world, she ached for her oldest child thousands of miles away across the oceans striving to become an officer like his late father. At least he was on his path, as difficult and challenging as it was, but Andromeda knew it would be the making of her son. A son she was already fiercely proud of.

Her three other children right now were her focus. She had to do all she possibly could to give them a protective, nurturing environment. She could do it, she thought with a conviction she didn't know she had within her. It was strange, she mused, after losing her husband upon whom she had depended for everything including the parenting of their children.

Now that he was no more, she felt an insane protective need to help her children through their individual journeys, by being the best possible parent she could ever be. She had her flaws and imperfections like anybody else, but she would always strive to do her utmost best.

* * *

CHAPTER 68

TROUBLED YEARS

The next few years passed in a blur of events that had tried Andromeda's patience to breaking point. The increasing tensions between her youngest child and herself were gaining momentum.

Andromeda was a bundle of frayed nerves, rushing between the chores and administrating household matters. Her younger son was giving her plenty of cause for concern He was already getting into trouble at school for small indiscretions. Nothing he did escaped the notice of his teachers or the other children. He was fast gaining a reputation for all the being the most disruptive and disobedient amongst all the children in his school.

Andromeda had a daughter Cynthia who was on the autistic spectrum. She had been two years old and had come to live with her grandparents because facilities for special needs children and adults were few to almost non-existent back in Pakistan. Andromeda's father who loved children especially his grandchildren had made the decision with the approval of Andromeda's husband to bring his granddaughter back to the UK where she would live with them and attend a special school for children with learning disabilities.

Cynthia would have access to specialist support and treatment for her condition which was not curable but would at least give her a better quality of life than if she had stayed back in Pakistan with her parents To this Andromeda's husband had readily agreed seeing the advantages that this would bring his daughter he was happy to let Cynthia be taken under the wing of her grandparents. Andromeda was happy that her daughter was thriving and in the care of her parents until the death of her father changed everything

It saddened her that despite her parent's help and support at raising their daughter for years the animosity and conflicts aimed by her in laws at her parents had not lessened. If anything it had intensified, nothing she could do or say would cool their ardour. They had been hell bent on destroying Andromeda and her family's reputation even if it had meant breaking up the marriage. She had been a thorn in their side for too long. Fate had decreed otherwise before they could put any plan into action her husband had been taken away silencing them all forever.

***

CHAPTER 69

DEATH OF FATHER

Andromeda had moved in temporarily with her mother but following the wake of her father's death, in 2007, that dark day that had befallen her family, Andromeda found her world torn apart and the barely constructed life she was holding together after her husband's death, was once gain shattered.

Her father had been diagnosed with bowel cancer and given only 6 months to live. Upon receiving the shocking diagnosis father had been remarkably calm as the doctor looked at father with sympathetic eyes He had known father and the whole family for many years and had treated them over the years becoming an integral part of the family. Dr Jaswant was fond of his patient and felt saddened to see the devastating illness that had taken hold.

It was bowel cancer now in its final stages. It was incurable There was nothing more he could do to prevent the inevitable aside from managing the pain which was only going to worsen as the days passed His patient had borne the news with great sadness and remarkable dignity accepting his fate as the will of God Father had always been a deeply religious man and believed with conviction that whatever happened it was meant to be Death would come to us all one day he had told the doctor and now his time was up it seemed It had come for him There was no escaping its clutches.

Father had always been a man imbued with great optimism and a joy of life no matter what the situation. Now he was going to have to shoulder the huge weight of the doctors bleak prognosis all alone. His family could not know or even come to suspect his illness for it would devastate them all beyond measure especially his wife The poor woman would be lost without him as all father had ever done throughout his life was to protect and provide for her and the children Now she would not have a clue about anything as he had taken care of everything for her How would she carry on thought father feeling a surge of helpless despair wash over him and the jolting realisation of his approaching mortality .

He had bear the weight of his secret all alone as much as it was going to prove to be a huge struggle. He could not watch his family fall to pieces around him In more ways than one everyone had come to depend upon his goodwill and sound advice He felt distraught at the thought that he was about to leave them all His life had been fraught with many tests and tribulations but overall he had had a good life and he loved his children and wife so much that the thought of leaving them sent shock waves of pain and nausea as the illness continued to make its ravage onslaught around his body.

He informed no-one in his family of the bleak diagnosis. Instead Andromeda's father had carried on as normal with no-one suspecting anything. Surreptitiously he began to rearrange and settle his debts and sorts' affairs as his weight began to plummet as the illness began manifesting itself. Till the very end Father had put up a brave and stoic fight, remaining selfless and gracious until he breathed his last.

After the funeral, life returned to a new normal, life that would be marred with the huge absence that stared back at them and the gaping emptiness her father had left in their lives. He had been a formidable presence in all their lives, and outside the family, many mourned father's passing.

Andromeda's mother and siblings were wracked with grief for a while they had rallied together in the days that had led up to father's rapid decline. After the funeral bereft and numb with father's death each had returned to some semblance of normalcy resuming their lives, but it would never feel the same again without father

* * *

CHAPTER 70

AUGUST 2006, HOUSE HUNTING

Andromeda began to look for houses as she could not stay indefinitely with her mother and sister. They had enough to deal with, without having to worry about Andromeda and her children. They would only be extra mouths to feed and a huge responsibility for her parents. She had looked into several rental properties. The cheaper ones which were the only ones she could afford had turned out to be unsuitable and unfit to live in.

Eventually after a painstaking year of moving between houses and renting, Andromeda decide to purchase a house, with the money she had saved up for a deposit. It would be the last of her savings She had sold the house back in Pakistan aware that she had underpriced it, but desperation to leave had been at the forefront of her mind had completed her to take the step.

Apart from her son there was nothing else to keep her there any longer. She hoped once her constraining was complete she would see him again. Until then staying on with her children had stopped being an option long ago
It was no longer viable or safe She could not trust anybody much less count on anyone to assure the safety of her family It was too dangerous her children were young and it was now down to her to bring them back to England where she could offer them some degree of security and comfort in the place from where her roots had sprung.

* * *

CHAPTER 71

JULY 2007, COLLAPSED CEILING

It was a lovely home within reach of the schools and all local amenities she had some money from her husband's inheritance and had been able to pay for a deposit and mortgage the property. The monthly instalments were huge but she had been hoping that soon she would be able to secure a job and then everything would be fine.

They had just moved in after much upheaval. She did not have much in the first place and everything had to be bought from beds to tables to the basics. They would somehow manage, she thought optimistically.

On the day they had moved in. Andromeda had been arranging her kitchen utensils, when she heard the cries of the children, screaming and shouting. She went into the hallway to scold them. It was way past their bedtime. They were excited at the prospect of this new place which was to be their new home.

Andromeda was thankful to climb into bed after another tiring day. She could have fallen asleep standing up. Just as she had turned back the duvet sheet, there was a loud immense bang which startled her. It was terrifying, she jumped back in alarm as the children woken by the loud noise cried out from their rooms.

Did something explode, did she leave the gas on? Worse still, had someone broken in? This and a myriad of terrifying thoughts flooded her mind. Andromeda called her neighbours and told them she was afraid to go down in case there was an intruder. They calmed and reassured a frightened Andromeda and came to the door. Andromeda ran downstairs flung open the door looking a picture of fright as she clutched at her yellowed terry towelling robe.

Her neighbours entered the long narrow hall way and that is when she saw it. All three saw in horror, mouths agape, and the scene of carnage that met their eyes through the open kitchen door way that faced the hall. The entire kitchen ceiling had collapsed and a pile of rubble sat underneath the now gaping hole that led into the bathroom. It was a stroke of luck that no one had been present at the time, especially her children. She dreaded to think what may have happened.

Andromeda, needless to say, was mortified as were her shocked neighbours. However, they had discussed insurance at length and pacified Andromeda that if she was insured it would get sorted swiftly and not to worry.

She had then called her insurance company who had promptly sent out a 'loss adjustor'. This was a special designated person Andromeda learnt whose job was to follow procedure on behalf of the insurance company He had to thoroughly investigate and look for eventualities that invalidated insurance claims ultimately determining on whose side the liability lay Andromeda had been very unfortunate in that the stern faced loss adjustor had arrived at a decision only a few minutes into his visit and without any preamble he had delivered his damning verdict.

Despite the huge pile of debris and a hole in the rafters he had concluded that it was due to a pre-existing condition whereby leakage of water over a consistent time had caused the ceiling to collapse. Andromeda's feeble attempts to reason with the man telling him that she had been paying her insurance premiums continuously when she had bought the house met with unconcerned apathy As he gathered his papers together and placed them in his leather briefcase, the loss adjustor snapped the locks shut with a final definitive gesture and arose from his chair after getting Andromeda to sign a few forms he then bid her a curt farewell and left seeing himself out She stood and watched his retreating back still clutching a copy of the insurance form that bore her signature nullifying any indemnity that she had claimed for They would not be paying out on this occasion as she was wholly liable for the incident. It was an absolute outrage Andromeda thought, she had prided herself for paying her insurance on time It was after all for any eventualities as this Otherwise what was the point of having insurance She could feel the tears prick her eyes as she wiped them away furiously She had no choice but to get the builders in. She hoped and prayed that she could find someone who would agree to set up a payment plan with her for the costs.

Later she sat down at the wooden dining table with her head in her hands after reassuring her children who were looking panicked and alarmed at the sight of so much rubble and dust and broken plasterboard scattered over the small kitchen. Everything from kitchen utensils to the work tops were coated in a thick film of dust A great big gaping hole with bits of timber and ceiling hung over their heads affording a glimpse into the bathroom from whence the leak had come. Andromeda's heart plummeted this was going to be costly and she did not have the money for it she would have to take a loan as she had no choice.

The roof was eventually fixed as were the bathroom pipes replaced, but it had cost her twice as much due to the complete ineptitude and slovenly workmanship of a cowboy builder. He had been known to her father, and was a middle aged, wizened looking man who had been in the trade for over 2 decades. Yet he had managed to make a shambles of the job which he had extracted a hefty amount for, much to Andromeda's anger. She had to have the work redone by somebody else in the end at huge loss to her.

* * *

CHAPTER 72

SPIRALLING DEBT

Her problems thus had resurfaced once more. Over the course of the next few months, debts began to pile up into a mountain. She dreaded the arrival of the post each morning. Any letter that came through the letterbox could only spell bad news.

These days it was only creditors and collectors asking for money. What was she supposed to do? She was still searching for jobs whilst working two and she had a family on top of her financial woes with 4 hungry children to feed and clothe.

It was virtually impossible as she struggled to keep on top of her rather large mortgage payments. Getting a house maybe had not been a smart move, perhaps she should have rented. Then again, she was young, inexperienced and short of advice.

It pained her that she could not even turn to her family for advice and support. Granted that they all had their fair share of problems and ongoing struggles, but surely being able to sit down and know that she was not alone, would have been enough.

A kind word, a comforting presence, an invite even to her family home, given that they all lived in the small town for years, yet they may as well have been on the opposite ends of the earth.

Andromeda silently got on with life, amidst her struggles she did what she thought was right at the time, to the best of her understanding. Everything had happened so fast, her husband's death, getting her older child settled, wrapping up affairs abroad, the move back to the UK, followed by her father's death. She had barely time to catch her breath between all the events.

Leaving her parental home after her father had been buried was painful. Now her mother and she were widows, a sad coincidence. Mother's worries were increased and she fretted and stressed over how they would manage.

Having a jobless, widowed daughter and 3 children was going be an additional burden and 4 hungry mouths to feed. Somehow Andromeda had to leave and find a place of her own. She could not stay here for ever and impose on her grieving mother. At least her youngest sibling, a sister who had worked her way up to a glittering career in the field of cognitive science would take care of mother in addition to her work and study. This gave Andromeda a small measure of hope.

Mother and Andromeda had never seen eye to eye on many things, and especially following Andromeda's widowed state. Mother had left no doubt as to what she had expected Andromeda to do. She could hear the echoes of her in-laws she had left behind, the mother-in-law telling Andromeda in no uncertain terms that her life was ineffectually over, and she had nothing to live and work towards except raising her children. She had to quash her own ambitions had she any. Mother was no different in these sentiments.

Nothing Andromeda did or didn't do was met with approval, right down to her dress sense. Andromeda was admonished as not depicting her status which was that of a widow and she had to dress a certain way and behave in a certain way.

Mother's main concern and complaint was to be invisible to the opposite sex, and not engage in any conversations with men in case they got ideas. Her status had remained unchanged through the years Mother remained adamant and vigilant when it came to monitoring her daughter Andromeda could not roam around carelessly and recklessly without her parents or a trustworthy guardian.

Decency and humility were the hallmark of mother's training. She was very protective when it came to Andromeda and her sisters. This began with covering herself up and making sure nothing about her daughter's appearance was tempting to men. Mother did not trust them for a single second. Men as far as mother was concerned were programmed to give into illicit desires and spared no female with the exception of their mothers. She was not going to take any chances especially where Andromeda was concerned. For she had already begun to blossom into a beautiful young woman full of youthful energy and the vitality of life. Her daughter reminded her of her own long spent youth before she was married off at a very early age to Andromeda's father.

Andromeda loved her mother very much and her siblings. Unfortunately since her marriage at the early age of 15, they had drifted apart, and the fissures in their relationship were so deep and furrowed that chance would be a fine thing before they ever went back to being the same as they had been in her childhood years.

Andromeda had answered an ad in a paper for a rental property that sounded affordable and was not too far from her mother's home. The first property was a rental nearby advertised at £50.00 a week. This was cheap and she could afford it with her benefits she thought When she had arrived to view the house, she was alarmed. It was not what she had expected at all even for a cheap rental. Surely there was a law against renting houses in such a dilapidated state as the one she had just viewed.

The outside was in a horrific state of disrepair. What appeared to be front facing windows were instead bricked up with large unsightly breeze blocks. The front door was a just a piece of battered board roughly nailed to cover the doorway. She shook her head in disbelief, she had seen enough, if this was the exterior, she didn't have to wager what the inside must look like. It would be far worse she assumed. Wrinkling her nose in disgust the foul odour of rotting rubbish had left no doubt about its previous occupant's propensity for living in such filth like conditions. How could people live like that she wondered? Turning away in dismay, she had to continue looking elsewhere. Something would turn up eventually she was sure of it.

The search to find cheap rentals had led Andromeda to the most worn down, deprived areas, she could not believe existed in her town. A town where she had been born in and had lived all her life, yet it harboured many secrets that she was unaware of Andromeda found she was as unfamiliar with many of its dark winding streets and deprived areas as the people who now inhabited them. She was a stranger in her own town.

The town had gone down considerably slumping to levels never seen or heard of, hence houses, for those who could afford them were as cheap as chips.

Run down council estates, and anarchic neighbours met her everywhere she looked. The epidemic of gang warfare, drug culture and criminal activity was rife in the impoverished sectors of her town. It was simply difficult to find a good decent neighbourhood to bring up children unless you had the means and resources to do that.

Andromeda had rented a couple of houses on the suggestions of people she knew but they had turned out to be uninhabitable after a few days. She discovered one of the houses she rented infested with rodents as large as cats. She had informed the council, but they were too overworked, and understaffed to send anyone over straight away for vermin control. How landlords could charge unscrupulous rents for homes that were clearly unfit for human habitation, she had thought dejectedly. What was the difference between these rogue over charging landlords and vermin, both were predators looking to scavenge what they could.

After a while she had found a home that was reasonable to all extents and decided to take out a mortgage. She had come into a bit of inheritance money that would help with the initial deposit and a few months of repayments. By that time she was confident that's he would have found a job.

* * *

CHAPTER 73

RED LETTER REMINDERS

The house had been surveyed and all the boxes ticked, it would be perfect for her and her children and it was located next to all the amenities, schools, shops, hospital, and public transport. It was ideal.

She managed to resolve one issue only to be faced with another. It was either, damp infesting the dining room wall, or the cracks appearing in the poorly constructed extension that was once a garage but now converted into an extra downstairs bedroom by its former occupants. It was a continuous cycle of fix, repair, replace. How the surveyor's report failed to pick up on these baffled Andromeda.

Before she knew where all her money had gone, her savings had dwindled to the point she could no longer afford the mortgage repayments on her house.

She had bought the house with her limited savings as a deposit, hoping a decent job would help her make the payments each month. She had not envisaged the accompanying problems that would arise from moving into a new home. The previous occupants had done a decent job to make it aesthetically pleasing, concealing any potential existing problems in a clever fashion through some well-crafted decorating.

She had to be thrifty and budget wisely to get through the days as best as she could.

* * *

CHAPTER 74

SWISS CHEESE & COWBOY BUILDERS

She had had to hire builders, to make the home safe and secure for her family. That in itself had accrued substantial costs, materials, labour, the latter of which was quoted at an eye watering cost, no doubt further inflated by the builder's consistent demands for one thing or the other.

No one could possibly have foreseen the future, the bathroom roof collapse, the extra mounting costs in getting the leaky plumbing fixed and ceiling redone. It was never ending thought an exasperated Andromeda. The house was like a Swiss cheese riddled with problems that were just appearing without warning.

Like many of the car mechanics and other professions, Andromeda had had to deal with, she found that one problem would suddenly morph into a number of things that required immediate repairs or replacing. Having very little knowledge on the mechanics or workings of cars and plumbing and house repairs.

Andromeda had reluctantly agreed to the exorbitant costs, simply because she had no experience or anyone to tell her any different or advise her of cheaper options.

Andromeda contributed to filling their pockets against her better judgement whilst making a deeper dent in her own. It was always a gamble, wherever she turned, if she needed a handy man, a local trade's person, a gardener, a plumber, an electrician, and a joiner in one instance, the yellow pages before the advent of apps and online reviews, were no guarantee that they were meticulous. Often, contrary to the alluring ads presented in print, the jobs would be botched and have to be redone by a different person, who charged twice for fixing the botched mess in the first place.

Being a single woman, with no apparent nose for these things did not help her case in the slightest. Her naive demeanour, and plain ignorance was a magnet for trade's people who could carry out jobs at inflated prices without any qualms.

Andromeda had begun to eventually understand the concept of researching her own quotes and checking reviews beforehand, but not before she had already parted with a lot of her money. She still balked at the one time she had hired a paint to paint the large living room, and he had charged her £800.00 without materials. What had she been thinking she bemoaned herself? Now she could paint an entire house having learned the art, through rigorous evening classes at her local college. She could do the same job for less than half that amount including materials. Oh well you live and learn, she told herself, vowing never to do anything so stupid again.

They were not perturbed in the slightest in skimming extra profit from customers. Rarely was the work done to a standard that justified the costs. Andromeda discovered things were slipping from her grasp, it was not long before she found herself drowning in debts. She had taken her finger off of the button and her finances had spiralled into a downward spin. She had some money in savings that were to keep her mortgage payments going until she got a better job.

She had two jobs which paid a pittance, given her lack of skills and qualifications, she was not employable material as yet She needed to gain some skills and experience before any employer took her seriously she thought disheartened at the thought This meant she had to find volunteer work and perhaps gain entry to some short term college courses that would get her the necessary qualifications Getting a job any job was proving to be far less easier than she had initially thought. Employers sought references something she did not have at this moment in time.

* * *

CHAPTER 75

BENEFITS

She managed to get state help, but her sense of propriety and dignity did not allow Andromeda to depend on the state infinitely. She had to do something to better her circumstances and break free from the chain of dependency on benefits.

The cliché, single mom, council house benefits, did not sit well with her. She was determined not to become another statistic. Lost in the system, engulfed by poverty, and reliant on state handouts for the rest of her life when she was more than capable of changing her situation. Her conscience simply would not allow her to fall in the trap.

With her new-found confidence, Andromeda was determined more than ever, that she would educate her way out of her status quo.

The first port of call was the job centre and, there the advisors would help her to make a CV. For now, she had a blank piece of paper with nothing but her name and address to show.

Today something as mundane as making a CV is easily created at the tap of a button on a computer keyboard. With everything readily accessible on the internet, access to technology and a plethora of resources, it enabled people to find jobs and create their individual profiles online without having to move from the cushy confines of their homes even.

Andromeda however given her lack of education, was not so tech savvy nor familiar with the basic rudiments of computing, let alone making a CV.

It had come as little to no surprise that from the age of 15 when she married, any development or progress in education was halted until the moment she became a widow. She had to restart the clock of learning and train herself in order to enter the world of work and employment.

Her children's survival depended upon her succeeding to that end. It was such a shame that she was unable to glean any support or comfort for that matter from her siblings who lived only a few streets away.

No one had ever visited or called her, though she had tried unsuccessfully to bridge the gaps that had widened over the years. They remained stoic and unmoved by her predicament, choosing to remain silent and hidden from sight.

This had only served to intensify her stigma, she was to all purposes an untouchable not only to society but to her own flesh and blood.

If Andromeda was going to break the chain of dependency on benefits and social security, she knew what she had to do. Getting a solid education and learning various skills along the way as she embarked upon the path of learning was her only ticket out of poverty. There were no short cuts to hard work and doing some drafting in order to have a comfortable life Those days when her husband had provided for them, with all the creature comforts that had accompanied his profession were long gone. She had to start afresh.

* * *

CHAPTER 76

CATCH 22, 2006

Getting a job, any job was going to be an arduous uphill task, she thought glumly. Her parents had never been keen on Andromeda completing her education. Getting their daughter married before she was indoctrinated by the Western culture was on their high list of priorities. They had meant well, but came from a school of dated cultural practices that saw girls married at a young age and started families when they were barely out of teens themselves.

Here she was at 31 widowed, mother of 4, lacking in skills, experience and an educational repertoire that extended only as far as high school. That too had been deeply affected by her fractious home life. Her parents' ongoing battles, arguments and fights had spilt over, creating a toxic environment for her. Mother was very unhappy, and many of her frustrations and anger were meted out on Andromeda.

She could not do anything right as far as mother was concerned. Going to school was her escape, a respite for a few hours until she ventured back home, where comfort, affection, a warm welcome were mere fantasies she harboured in her head.

In spite of that, she had managed to scrape through school with a few GCSE's and some failed grades. It was all she had to show for her depth of knowledge. She loved to read and had nurtured that passion whenever she had an opportunity. At home, her mother assigned tasks around the house which Andromeda did diligently and without question.

She feared her mother's wrath. Father by contrast was a gentile, patient soul, 17 years his wife's senior, but he was tolerant to a fault. He was often at the receiving end of her mother's rebukes

If housekeeping and being a mother in addition to catering to her in-laws ever present demands for years counted, then she had an impressive record of 16 years' experience.

Upon becoming a very young parent and a housewife, she had to learn through mistakes, trial and error. There had been no training manual, or advice or pep talk and crash courses given. Simply, Andromeda had been thrown in at the very deep end. Although many of her efforts in her marital home had gone unnoticed and unacknowledged. She had been a means to an end as it turned out.

* * *

CHAPTER 77

JOB SEEKER 2007

Having wandered dejectedly through the dank smelling, musty corridors of various employment recruitment agencies and job centres over the years, Andromeda came to understand the mechanisms of the job work search environment.

It was a huge wake up call for her at any rate not to mention a painful lesson in humility and self-preservation.
It must be a minefield for the advisors Andromeda thought overwhelmed at the scenes that greeted her each time she visited the job centre There was a constant flux of people and irate job seekers from the old, the young, the sick, the elderly even the work-shy individuals who concocted creative excuses to avoid work but ensured they received their job seeker giros each week. Here one could find people from all walks of life downtrodden and crippled by financial constraints of some kind united in their quest to secure employment that would liberate them from economic woes.

Andromeda witnessed it all from her vantage point at every appointment, when she would arrive half an hour earlier than her appointment time. She was afraid of being late and having sanctions imposed on her. Something she could ill afford right now.

Andromeda gasped at the plethora of people who came here. Each encumbered with their own personal burdens and battling poverty, come through these doors expecting or hoping to find the answer to all their problems.

Over the months and years, Andromeda had found herself more than once battling poverty, fighting hardship, raising three children as a single parent. No one wanted to hire her. She simply had no skills, no experience, and no job. Nothing that would endear her to prospective employers. She saw her job coach every fortnight who helped Andromeda to navigate her way through potential life skill courses and job opportunities. It was a minefield of prospects out there, but she was raw and unemployable.

Security guards were a now permanent feature of most job centres. These burly no-nonsense towering beef eaters graced the lobby and hallways of the rooms watching with hawk eyed vision for any sign or whiff of trouble. Trouble was in full supply she noted with bemusement as she sat and waited for her appointments each week.

Tensions flared, jobseekers, weighted by their individual burdens, the dispassionate and resigned losing faces dotted about in the open waiting areas where a line of desks placed horizontally along both sides of a long hall, each awaiting their turn to be called, some clutching wrinkled, folded up CVs, single mothers wielding prams and followed by a couple of bedraggled children, bored and fidgety in this oppressive hall.

Hushed sounds and barely perceptible conversations are discernible to the inquisitive ear. From the booths, one can hear the presence of the security guards pacing up and down, occasionally signposting new job seekers to where they are meant to go, placating and a silent message to the public to uphold the rules and regulations in this building. Public disorder of any kind was not up for discussion. That was the strong message they imparted.

It was an interesting place to watch the various interactions and complex emotions on display. The sheer utter desperation on these people's faces mirrored her own, Andromeda noted with wistfulness.

The employees at the job centre spent copious hours sifting through the tons of CV applications, updating records and helping match job hunters to appropriate jobs. They too had a set rota of goals to accomplish which meant getting more jobseekers into paid employment. Their jobs were also on line if they fell short of the mark.

It was a common sight to watch each interviewer discussing at extraordinary length with their jobseeker client, as she watched with interest, the buzz of different conversations emanating from each cubicle packed side by side composed of a desk and Computer with which each advisor turned to indicate something to their appointee.

She approached Thursdays with dread and rising panic when the clock struck 9, hiding in the shadows not wanting to be seen by other members of the waiting public, not wanting to catch the eyes of the keenly scanned visionary tentacles of its staff, puffed out chests and immaculate crisp white uniforms assuming the self-importance of public servants poised and ready to dispense justice on tiny rowdy or unhinged jobseekers.

As she reluctantly shuffled across the faded patterned floor of the job centre casting nervous glances around me, Andromeda felt sick to the stomach. She had an appointment with her work coach and as the time drew close, she grew more nervous, shifting uneasily in her seat.

It was a bee hive of activity with an array of cluttered desks lined up along both sides of the job centre manned by stern looking advisors, hunched up in front of their dated computer terminals, gazes glued to the screens, as they navigated the mouse to different pages ready to receive their next appointment.

The odd shouts could be heard above the constant hum and buzz of people, From somewhere behind a partition screen an indignant protest would rise up quelled just as swiftly by the burly security guards positioned within hearing distance a sweeping the crowded floor with hawk steely eyed vision on the lookout for trouble.

In that time as a job seeker, Andromeda had had a few different coaches all with the single-minded focus to get her on the employment ladder.

The job market was a minefield of jobs but Andromeda found to her despair that every time, she ran headlong into the same problem. For many of the roles she applied for, where she managed to fit the skills criteria, she was sorely lacking in experience. It was a catch 22 not to mention incredibly frustrating.

As a job seeker, her commitments included trawling through countless job sites, subscribing too many, e-mailing potential employers and reporting to her local job centre, every two weeks to update them of her frequent searches and demonstrating her efforts to become employed.

* * *

CHAPTER 78

FOOT IN THE DOOR

Every week as she trudged through the rain sleet and snow in all weathers to join the lowly crowd of fellow jobseekers. The air was filled with the desolate acrid stench of desperation and sheer hopelessness.

Clutching her little appointment card, she glanced about nervously taking in the pinched sad faces of the people who flocked to the government building.

The pungent stench of unwashed bodies and acrid sweat fills one's nostrils, as humanity lost and forlorn, all victims of some circumstances or the other stride purposefully through the swing doors. All the while her son was spiralling into a destructive pattern of behaviour. Andromeda fought to keep money coming in, through a rigorous routine of jobs, night classes, volunteer work to better her chances.

She was walking a double-edged sword, trying to make ends meet while trying to raise her family. Her son was unhinged and hampering her effort but she ploughed through the day and night, trying to keep her emotions at bay. There was no time for self-reflection or self-pity, she was tired but more tired of her son's unruly antics that were affecting the whole family.

The unmistakable stale smell of tobacco and often alcohol is not lost on her senses which are under attack. The prickle of self-consciousness reminded her why she was there and increased her anxiety at meeting her job coach.

A perpetual cycle of giro, booze, cigarettes, drugs follow
before the next appointment as jobs are hard to come by
and if there are jobs then they ask for experience.

* * *

CHAPTER 79

THE JOB COACH

Why was it that she always felt these seemingly ordinary people exuded powers and control beyond my reach? As her name was called, I would break out in beads of sweat and experience pin pricks of irritation, crawling like a thousand little ants up her skin.

Her heart would be palpitating and my mouth dry as she sat down, and obediently like a child at junior school, both in awe and intimidated by authority. She was probably older than the young wiry man in front of her who looked like he had just graduated High School.

Andromeda was never good with authority and felt my confidence plummet each time she was confronted by those in a position of responsibility that practically included everyone.

As the young bored looking man asked Andromeda questions, same scripted ones he was compelled to as part of his job, her agitation increased tenfold.

She had never felt so incompetent, unskilled, inarticulate, and unimportant, then at this moment. Being questioned at these interviews on her progress of job hunting reminded her of school, where her lack of confidence with teachers instilled terror when questioned by figures of authority.

In order to get the giro to feed my children, I had to work for it by being here every two weeks as mortifying as it was each time for me.

Over the course the next few months Andromeda's job coaches changed. Each time she visited there would be different people but at one point she had the same job coach for a few weeks who had been very helpful and supportive

For the most part the job advisors were helpful, and compassionate, towards the jobseekers that flocked through the revolving doors. This was important as many of them came from dire situations and broken families like herself. Their desperation and misery was clearly etched upon their worn and haggard looking countenances

Almost straight away Andromeda had felt out of place and uncertain about herself She had nothing to her credit that could get her gainful employment She was as raw as they came The only skills she had if they could be counted were those that came from life and the school of hard knocks All that she had learned had come from everything life had thrown her way a married woman, housewife and mother That would not get her very far she had thought despondently

One advisor had not bothered to conceal her disdain as she looked down her bespectacled face condescendingly She did not have to say it but her disapproval was obvious from her impression reflecting back at Andromeda her ineptitude to have secured any job at all. She probably regarded her as just another cliched good for nothing single mother siphoning off the state and living comfortably off benefits rather than work for a living The blatant discrimination was written in the advisor's eyes Andromeda fought to hold back tears because she knew she was anything but a lazy sponger of benefits Circumstances and desperation had driven her to this place She had little choice until she was back on her feet again.

There had been a week in which Andromeda had been appointed a different advisor He was a churlish and very matter of fact gentleman whose volley of questions put Andromeda's teeth on edge. She was barely given a chance to respond as he barraged her with a volley of information the clear implications being that she should settle for any job they found for her They did not want any excuses no matter what her situation Child care was a concern even though her children were not toddlers but they were still minors and she needed a job to fit around their school timings

She was already nervous as she approached the cubicle where her job advisor sat waiting with a touch of annoyance and impatience.

The stern impassive looking job coach wasn't helping ease her mounting anxiety. Almost accusatory, she felt the keen questioning eyes silently saying, "Well, what excuse do we have this time?" Why are you not working? This time she had come prepared, taking out her diary where she had noted, times, dates, and job applications she had sent off in the last 2 weeks, and the polite rejections received in response.

This seemed to appease the coach who nodded approvingly. After giving Andromeda some more information, the appointment ended and she was internally relived that she could relax for another 2 weeks at least Somehow the trips to the job centre left her feeling beleaguered as if she had been placed on trial each time walking away with a feeling of guilt at not securing a job.

She had also tried a stint at a nursing home for seniors. Andromeda found herself out of sorts at first but eventually settled in once she got to know the elderly residents. They were lovely and touched her to the core especially the vulnerable and frail service users. Andromeda was deeply affected by many of their stories, and unsurprisingly struggled to remain objective. A month had barely passed and they had to let her go citing budgetary issues. Every two weeks that Andromeda was summoned to the job centre, her stomach recoiled in dread at the mere thought of it.

She was sorely out of her depth in this strange place. She looked nervously upon the friendly countenance of the lady sat across from her, possibly in her late 40s.

The employees here, had impossible targets to meet, that one could not help feeling a sense of sympathy for them. It would be nigh on impossible with the huge unemployment market as it stood, with hordes of people flocking through their busy doors daily. They had set targets and quotas to complete which involved getting as many applicants off the jobseekers' benefit and into employment.

Andromeda gulped down a rising sense of self-pity and felt nauseous. Here she was, a widow, a place she never imagined she would end up in. Her husband had provided for quite comfortably, she had never wanted for anything and now here she was dependent upon handouts from the state to feed her family.

After countless days and nights, working on an old battered computer, she had managed to get second hand and for a considerable discount Andromeda managed to create her CV. Although it was glaringly empty, there was nothing to put on it apart from her personal details. There was no experience or employment history to put on. Since leaving school, all she had known for 16 years was being a wife and a mother. For the rest she was utterly clueless about life in the work place.

* * *

CHAPTER 80

"YOU ARE NOT QUALIFIED ENOUGH"

After many rejections, and failures at her complete lack of skills and experience, she had decided to enrol on an Open University Course. It was going to be a continuous uphill struggle she knew that with mounting dread, 8 years of online studies and 4 children to raise. Managing her home on very little, with next to nothing. She had no savings, no money, nothing. Life was filled with hurdles at every juncture. Somehow, she had successfully completed the degree, although she knew she could have done better but, having to juggle single parenting duties, and her late night studies meant that her already dwindling energy reserves were fading.

She had followed up her university studies with a diploma and extra night classes to build her skill set in a mixed bag of subjects. Yet she always faced the incongruous task of accepting rejections. If she had the qualifications, she lacked experience.

Over the months that followed Andromeda had started attending night classes and even day classes where possible to cover her basic skill deficiencies. It was hard with the children, but somehow she managed to gain a few qualifications, including a basic computer course that would stand her in good stead. She even managed a few classes in French only for the simple reason that she enjoyed the whole learning process and got to meet other people outside the home.

With the hindsight of life experience, behind her and slightly more wisdom than she had been imbued with in her youth, Andromeda launched herself eagerly into this new phase of her life. Reinventing herself, despite having the responsibility of her children, developing a confidence she barely recognised in herself, and cultivating strong friendships, meant the tide was finally turning.

She had to find the time and energy to focus on her own personal development. It was the only way she could be guaranteed a job in the future. The classes were a welcome reprieve Andromeda found herself enjoying every minute. Returning to education later on in life after a long hiatus proved to be far less daunting than she had originally feared.

Once she had mastered the basics in using a computer, Andromeda had set herself the task of creating several profiles on job search sites. Something would come back she was sure, although many she did apply for resulted in failure as she did not match the criteria.

Filled with disappointment, Andromeda refused to be deterred, she would take whatever she could in different fields widening her options. Volunteering with organisations like the British Red Cross, the Citizen's advice bureau would greatly increase her chances and enhance her skills, Andromeda thought. She had to start somewhere, doing nothing was not an option.

* * *

CHAPTER 81

FIRST JOB, BANK HALL, LANCASHIRE

Andromeda had been offered a place to work part time at a nursing home for the elderly. It was not too far from her home, and the hours were flexible. It was daunting at first as she had never had a job before. This was her first step in a work environment. She felt grossly out of her depth. The staff were friendly and accommodating, and the jobs assigned to Andromeda were carefully monitored, and she was always teamed up with another staff member so the probability of making mistakes was reduced.

She found the residents endearing, and enjoyed caring for them as she settled in. It was an eye-opening experience to encounter the fragility and vulnerability of the residents. They were old, and many had afflictions which were heartbreaking, as they neared the end of their lives, many had little to no families on the outside who visited frequently.

Andromeda felt a surge of affection and love with each of her patients. They were a lot of protocols, and rules she had to follow and adhere to. Remaining objective and desensitised was the hardest one to follow. She found it immensely rewarding to engage and bring a smile to their faces as they welcomed her and enjoyed her company and regaled Andromeda with their countless stories. Some bore painful scars and found Andromeda to be a welcome reprieve to their otherwise joyless hours in the home. There was one patient, an elderly lady in her 80s who had told Andromeda she was like a daughter she had never had.

There was no greater compliment than that to be had, Andromeda thought with a surge of affection and empathy for the dear resident.

The days passed by in a blur of activities and learning on the job. Andromeda loved every second and discovered that she could see herself in any caring profession, like this. It was immensely fulfilling and not to mention rewarding to be able to make a positive difference in people lives. At meal times, Andromeda would help feed the more severely impaired residents.

They were like children for her except they had a plethora of life experiences behind them and advancing years, but age had regressed to a childlike vulnerability.

Andromeda felt blessed to be in a position to help them.

Unfortunately her joy was short-lived as she was summoned by her superior just days before her contract was coming to an end. Carla her manager informed Andromeda due to the economic crisis, they had to let go of some of their staff which included Andromeda. It was always the case in the job sector, last one in, first one out.

They were very sorry to see her go and reassured Andromeda that she could come back when new positions were available in the future.

Their words did little to comfort however as she left the office she had come to love so much She had never felt important or proud of herself that she worked in a job that made a difference to people's lives It had not been a well-paid job and the hours were too few but it had been a start a huge step up for Andromeda who knew how much she had had to struggle to get to this position.

She had worked night and day to build her cv with lots of volunteering experience at the local advisory bureau She had loved every second of it The fact that she was not paid for her time as a volunteer had been difficult because money was already tight However she had remained steadfast in her decision to keep going and to plough forwards

Her local job centre which she had to attend fortnightly in search of employment had brought this position to her attention She had needed no skills or qualifications for the role

Now she had to waive everything away and say goodbye with a heavy heart. Saying goodbye too many of the residents whom she had come to adore and forge close knit bonds was upsetting, but as she was discovering, this was the real world of employment. Anything could happen, jobs came and jobs went. It was normal. Remaining impartial and objective as well as professional were key concepts she would do well to remember.

* * *

CHAPTER 82

RETAIL PASSPORT BOOTSTRAP

Andromeda trudged through the pebbled dash way leading to the main door of the local job centre for her fortnightly appointment. She was back to the drawing board she thought wistfully, after a brief but successful stint at her first job. She had learned a lot in the six months' time she had been employed. The joy of earning her first ever pay check on her own merit, learning to work alongside colleagues and work staff, the camaraderie that existed in the work place. It had been a huge learning curve.

Today her job coach was a fresh faced young man who looked barely older than her son and just out of college His youthful appearance however didn't detract from his effectiveness as he highlighted several options and signposted Andromeda to a course he thought, she would notably benefit from but it would help her get gainful employment which of course was the ultimate goal. She was to attend a 4 week course to get a formal certificate and what was known as a "retail passport' which would then be used to secure a position in any retail outlet. It was a different job to caring in a nursing home, but it was still a job at the end of the day Andromeda thought, and many of the rules that applied would be the same.

It was not rocket science learning the basics of working in retail. The course itself, was delivered by a tall statuesque looking female instructor. She was very enthusiastic and exuded style and grace as she put our class of 8 women through their paces.

A guaranteed internship or apprentice ship with any retail outlet was waiting for each of the students once we had completed the work and maintained full attendance.

The possibly of getting a paid contract after an apprenticeship through the scheme known as Bootstrap was more likely than applying by themselves.

* * *

CHAPTER 83

SECOND JOB, NEXT COLNE

After the course, Andromeda was delighted to learn she would sent to the Next Retail store, a famous British multinational clothing and footwear retailer.

Andromeda started working as soon as he had received her retail passport, proud of herself that she had started making small inroads to the achievement of her goals. Every small victory felt like a huge success to her. She had managed to save her home, rid herself of the debt, the children were settling into their school life. Andromeda was learning about life in the employments sector. She continued toward at Next after a successful 4 week probationary period, she was offered a 6 month contract, renewable every 6 months.

Working on the ground floor the women's department enabled Andromeda to interacted customers, offering customer service, stock taking, and selling products. In time she came to love her job, although the hours were long, but gratifying, as Andromeda found she connected well with her customers, who specifically asked after her on her days off. Some of her regular customers chose to drop by on the days she was working which was heartwarming.

She loved being around people and communicating with others, which made her sociable and easy to approach. It did feel a little strange at first to note that the staff, in senior positions and the junior employees were younger than Andromeda when she had first arrived.

Taking instructions and orders from her juniors was odd, but she had gotten used to it. She had come to do her first jobs at an age where people were far along in their careers, having started out young. Andromeda had arrived at this point via a circuitous route instead, with more life experiences than her much younger fellow employees. She was more ahead in that regard, the rest she had to relearn and reinvent herself to be successful in the employment world.

Her children were now in their teens. Both her daughters were over 18 and Andromeda relied more on her younger daughter to hold the fort and watch over her siblings until she got home. Andromeda worked 9 hours whatever her work gave her, she gladly accepted. It was exhausting for someone who had never worked long hours, but she was happy that she had learned to become independent, find her way around. On top of that she was now actually earning an income.

As in her previous job, every month upon receiving her payslip, she felt a surge of pride and happiness, that she had earned her own money and could now support her family. It was something that she could never have envisaged in her previous life. Holding her pay checks in her hand, gave her a strong immeasurable sense of empowerment. It was amazing. At this rate she could almost envision her dream of reaching heights in the pulsating job market.

As long as she never stopped learning and kept her wits about her. She would be able to ensure stability and financial security for her children.

* * *

CHAPTER 84

EVICTION NOTICE

Despite having taken out home insurance against such unforeseen eventualities, her insurance company rejected her claim. The loss adjustor a cunning looking man who had turned up at Andromeda's home to assess the damage, was undaunted by the apparent pile of rubble that covered half of the small kitchen, remnants of the collapsed ceiling. Above his head, he could see the gaping hole leading into the bathroom.

As a distraught Andromeda tried to explain how it had happened and without warning, the loss adjustor merely shook his head, a solemn expression on his face giving away nothing, he had jotted a few notes in his leather bound diary and said they would be in touch. Loss adjustors to Andromeda's knowledge were designated to investigate between loss and fraudulent claims.

It was as she had feared, the claim was denied. There was no plausible reason. It was a no brainer. The investigator had cunningly used a loophole that would prevent Andromeda's insurers paying out her claim.

They had found one, a discreet one line buried beneath reams of high falutin paragraphs citing "that there was reasonable evidence to suggest a pre-existing condition in the property before Andromeda had moved in, in layman's terms "a leak" that had caused the ceiling to collapse. Andromeda had moaned in despair and utter disbelief. She had paid for an initial surveyor to inspect the property for any underlying faults and defects before making the purchase. Clearly her case was cut and dry. To top it all her insurance had used a clever ploy to deny paying

Andromeda anything to cover her damage. It was time to change insurers, she decided dejectedly.

This was how some insurance companies made their profits, she thought ruefully. It pained her to realise that her meagre savings would now have to go on repairs leaving her with a significant shortfall to manage the rest of the bills. How was she going to keep up with her repayments?

* * *

CHAPTER 85

MORTGAGE RESCUE SCHEME – END IN SIGHT

Just as expected, a few days later the letters began arriving, in earnest the reminders, the default notices, with huge capital red letters emblazoned across the front, in case she missed the message contained inside, debt agency letters followed, and then the calls from the bank. She was behind with her mortgage by a few months.

It had got to the point that upon waking up, Andromeda dreaded the sound of the postman posting the letters through the flap, the rustle of the envelopes as they fell onto the mat inside the door. She wanted to avoid opening her letters, filled with a sick dread coiling up as a sinking feeling descended in her stomach. She had thought at this point she would have been able to secure a job of some sorts. They had been in the house for 8 months. The job hunting process was taking longer than she had thought.

Finally the letters of default, and threat of action began to arrive each day. Proceedings were now in full force and eviction was imminent. Andromeda's panic had scaled new heights as her anxiety deepened. She knew without a doubt that she was going to lose her home.

Citizen's advice bureau TO THE RESCUE.

Andromeda decided to visit her local citizens advice bureau, someone at work had mentioned it to her in passing and told her that she could get some much needed support and advice especially regarding her debt situation which they could help her with.

At this point, Andromeda was dejected, lost and in total despair.

She had almost gotten used to the rejections, by now. It was hardly a surprise given that she had next to nothing to bring to the table. She was a blank canvas with little outward appeal for employers.

It was Tuesday, a blustery day as the rain drizzled down, and a cold wind engulfed her thin frame. Andromeda clutched her jacket tighter around her. She had dropped the children off at school. Today she was going pay her local citizens advice bureau a visit. She had no idea what to expect. It was now or never. She was a mess of nerves after having received a date for the actual repossession of her home.

It was less than 5 days away, in which she and her children would be on the street unless she secured accommodation for themselves soon.

She headed with determined strides towards the multi office building housing many small offices for different businesses. There was a nondescript room to one side, with leaflets attached to a wooden board. This must be it she thought, taking in the musty smell of the stuffy, reception area. There were a few chairs lined up against the walls.

She tentatively approached the desk where the receptionist sat, talking into a phone, as she jotted down some information, before hanging up. Andromeda took in the features of the woman, pleasant looking and friendly, supporting, and short black cropped hair in a pixie cut that complimented her face. The woman wore brightly a coloured dress with a geometric print and a string of large beads to match her equally large ear rings. She greeted

Andromeda with a warm smile, instantly putting the young woman at ease, and asked how she could help.

Andromeda explained she wanted to see a debt advisor and was then ushered towards a seat in the small cramped waiting room, until summoned. She had time to take in her surroundings which looked quite shabby and unkempt, there were a few clients waiting looking sad and forlorn as Andromeda.

Sadness and hopelessness seemed to permeate the walls of the room, clinging to the unadorned walls. For many who sought the help and advice of the CAB, it was a last resort, and a place that could offer them some semblance of hope in their dire predicaments of life. In these despondent waiting rooms, people were united by the same goal. Each individual sought a resolution and advice that would break the cycle of despair which most people had become entangled in.

It brought a small measure of relief to Andromeda to know that, she was far from alone in her troubles.

They were those who were much worse off, and to this she should count herself lucky. People who had nothing to eat, and were living in abject poverty, came here to access food banks, others, were embroiled in abusive relationships and sought refuge, there were those who simply sought justice for a wrong done to them and they wanted help to be heard.

A stale smell undisguised by the use of air fresheners hung stoically in the atmosphere. All manner and descriptor people would come through the doors, unkempt, unwashed, or too troubled to care, it was not uncommon to see people in the throes of hardship and burdened with all the troubles of the world walk in to this unimpressive office hoping against hope that therein beyond these little cubicles was the answer to their problems.

She sat nervously squirming in her chair casting tentative glances surreptitiously all around feeling a wave of guilt and inadequacy was over her. She felt wracked with guilt, pervading every ounce of her body, reminding her accusingly that she was here because of her own failings to cope with her situation.

Her hopeless inadequacy mocked and jeered at her inability because she lacked the resources to help her get her life back on track.

Being a widowed single parent was presenting momentous obstacles and challenges. She felt like she was drowning in a sea of utter hopelessness.

It was a perpetual cycle of hopelessness and futility she seemed to be going around in. No qualifications or experience, meant no job, hence no money to survive on. Bills that needs paying and children to raise. Any training to get onto the job market would cost money she didn't have in the first place, and childcare was an option she could ill afford.

The result was that debts had accrued, and eviction from her home was imminent unless providence intervened. Maybe just maybe as she glanced at the peeling magnolia walls casting a sickly hue over the waiting room, this was her last chance before.

Today was the day Andromeda would finally put her plan into motion. Today she was going to end this situation one way or the other, as continuing was no longer an option. She would take whatever drastic steps at whatever cost if it meant it afforded her children a better chance of survival from their poverty afflicted status. A way out of their currant hardship she thought. Her children had to thrive at all costs and she was not going to stop until she had exhausted every option, and every possibility.

Graham listened attentively... a soft expression on his worn rough hewn features. He was a balding man of 50 plus years who had served with the bureau for over a decade was one of the most experienced of the team there, and knew a thing or two about the sheer desperation and hopelessness that propelled people to his agency. A place of last resort for many.

There was nothing more rewarding than finding workable solutions and watching the grief and distress leave his clients faces as they were given a lifeline to the problems which a moment before had threatened to engulf them.
He too had suffered his fair share of traumatic experiences in life that had shaped and strengthened him eventually. To be able to give back a little to society was the very least Graham felt he could do, and help those afflicted and struggling to cope. It was his way of giving back, paying it forward.

He looked up from his modest desk on which sat an untidy pile of case notes and a very outdated but working computer, next to which sat his chipped mug of now cold tea.

Graham could clearly see a woman in turmoil and it was difficult not to be moved by her dishevelled and disoriented state. This woman clearly looked depressed, judging by her lacklustre appearance, Graham thought pondering at his client, who fidgeted nervously in her chair. The advisor was talking to her in a soothing way beckoning Andromeda to take a seat on the not so comfortable chairs but she appeared to be distracted, as her gaze settled upon the train tracks beyond the window. The gloomy dismal scene outside only enhanced her own sense of despair.

A twisting winding mass of corrugated steel tracks and fixtures, dull, and lifeless as she felt. This picture, devoid of colour, painted an all too depressing scene which beckoned to Andromeda.

She looked wistfully outside the old sash window of her stuffy surroundings with its, chipped, white peeling paint on the sides, she noticed how the tracks looked deserted, with the odd train rumbling past ferrying its cargo of bored, commuters.

That would be ideal she thought, no witnesses, or inquisitive passer bus or dog walkers to try and apprehend her intentions. It would be quick, simple and painless, she mused. Life had taught her that she did not belong here, in fact she did not want to be here now. Her mind, wrestled and competed with conflicting thoughts as, the voice of reason grappled with her dark twisted voice of doom, that all was lost.

Her numbed brain tried to make sense all the sense as she jostled to wrench herself back to her present surroundings with start she looked up when Graham emitted a cough to bring her back from her momentary state of reverie. She continued to glance furtive looks towards the window at the train tracks, her hands were trembled as she clasped and unclasped them he noted with alarm. What was her story? He was about to find out.

He could sense the enormity of this young woman's situation. Her distress was palpable and heartbreaking to watch. She was a mess and only Lord knew what had happened to bring this woman to such a plight.
He fetched her a glass of water to help calm her before they began. He was eager to find out what why she was here. He had dealt with many clients but not half as troubled and in worse shape as this uncertain looking woman in his office. She looked like she was on the verge of collapse judging by her nervous disposition.

He listened intently, placed some calls, listened more and then proceeded to put a plan into action with immediate effect. After several interminably long conversations on the phone, he had turned to look at Andromeda with an encouraging nod, and explained that he had managed get her approved for the Mortgage Rescue scheme, a project that had been rolled out nationwide, and had recently come to their attention. It was in its pilot stages but Graham assured Andromeda that she would be the first one to benefit from the scheme. Plans were being put into motion.

The Mortgage Rescue would lease with her bank from today, and buy the house, clearing her mortgage, arrears and all. The house would be sold to a housing association, who would then rent the house to Andromeda, enabling her to continue to stay in her home but as housing tenant. She would receive all the necessary help with rent allowing her to focus on getting back on her feet.

Andromeda was speechless, as she felt fresh tears prick her eyes. She could not formulate the words to say thank you. She didn't have to. Graham understood. He was delighted for her. The young woman who sat opposite him had been through a rough patch and deserved some good news at last. He was happy for her.

They finally said goodbye and an enigmatic Andromeda left the building, feeling light hearted and elated. Thank you God, she said looking up.

In the nick of time Andromeda had managed to save her family from being evicted and made homeless. They had been days from being turned out of their home until the intervention of the Citizen's Advice Bureau.

With a palpable sigh of relief, she felt a huge burden lift from her, the weight of worries had mounted and piled up over the years until she felt she was going to collapse from exhaustion. Now at least Andromeda could see a flicker of hope along the horizon. Maybe this scheme which the advisor was now checking up on as he placed a few phone calls would be the answer she was looking for.

Andromeda felt herself visibly and mentally relaxed for now. She could now look forward to a good night's sleep, something which her senses and body had long been deprived of.

* * *

CHAPTER 86

REPOSSESSION HALTED

They were assured of a roof over their head for now and the huge debt was gone. Her children were safe for now. Although they no longer owned the house the housing association who had stepped into purchase it, had rented it back to Andromeda, clearing the huge debt and providing additional support in which she was able to rent from them instead. Her relief was palpable in the knowledge that there would be no bailiffs knocking down her doors with possession orders to evict her. At least her children were now safe in the home.

The last eight months had been the most gruelling and painful as her debts had escalated The knowledge that her home would be repossessed had kept her awake for nights on end She had lost all hope and even her faith had begun to diminish as her prayers had gone unanswered until the days had walked into the citizen's advice bureau

Her life had been taken over by the clearly unmistakable threats contained within the dozens of letters that had poured in through her letterbox all from her creditors and her bank. She had never felt so helpless and hapless in her whole life a cornered prey waiting to be ripped apart and eaten alive by sharks. Having surrendered herself to the fate of homelessness and becoming destitute with her children in a few days from now when the eviction began.

She had not for a single second expected the sudden turn of events that would follow from her one visit to the CAB office. Nobody could have foreseen what happened after

One call from the advice office to her bank and a few other agencies had effectively halted the impending eviction and grounds to keep Andromeda and her children in her home had begun to take shape

The citizen's advice bureau had proven to be her saviour. She had no words, she was speechless not to mention immensely grateful.

She had managed to dodge a bullet for now. They were staying in their home.

* * *

CHAPTER 87

DERAILED YOUNGEST SON

Her younger son's activities and beginnings of his dysfunctional career took root. The house became a hot bed of anger, dissent, tensions.

The next few years proved to be tumultuous to say the least for Andromeda. Being a single parent was not cut and dried, and there was no right or wrong way to go about it. No matter which way the wind blew or what she did, it would not alter the outcome of what was meant to be. She tried to reason with herself that it was best to leave everything to fate Andromeda alone had no inkling at what lay ahead before her.

* * *

CHAPTER 88

AUTISTIC CHILD

Her daughter Cynthia had not been diagnosed until she was 3 years old. At the time Andromeda had never heard of the autistic spectrum or the general nature of the condition. Her daughter's paediatrician had told Andromeda that it was delayed milestones and severe "retardation "a term almost certainly banished from usage and considered derogatory in today's world.

The ensuing years had been fraught with difficulties in trying to understand her daughter's sudden outbursts and meltdowns. Andromeda was not equipped to recognise or handle the triggers that caused her daughter to lapse into fits which as time passed had only worsened.

She knew as did everyone who met Cynthia that she was different to all the other children. Her outlook, her physical and mental state did not match her chronological age, she seemed to lag behind in years and in developmental terms. Her siblings struggled to understand and cope with their 'different' sister. By the same coin, she struggled with all of them.

From an early age, Cynthia was finally taken out of her primary school and sent to a special needs school. Her abnormal behaviour had induced, fits of kicking screaming and biting her teachers, until eventually special help had been called in. Cynthia was issued with a SEN Statement of educational needs and for the next progressive years until the age of 16, she attended the special schools with children and young adults with learning disabilities.

Finally after months of painstaking effort, and negotiating with various agencies Andromeda had found an organisation willing to help her.

This was only after she had been signposted from one office to another buffeted from pillar to post until she found the correct agency who would take Cynthia's case The struggle was far from over as Andromeda discovered much to her dismay she had to fight and claw her way through the myriads of red tape and bureaucracy in which corporate and governmental organisations shrouded in Finally she was able to get the attention of the social services and the learning disabilities team.

Months of intense assessments, reviews and visits followed. Eventually Cynthia was offered the option of going into supported living. She was now 18 and classed as a young vulnerable adult with limited capacity. At least she would be in a protected environment surrounded by adults with special limiting needs and varying capacities.

Andromeda felt reassured and comforted by the fact that her daughter would be able to acquire independence whilst living alongside her peers and trained staff who would overlook and supervise them on a daily basis. She had tried at home and failed because her daughter's autism and limited needs had made it extremely difficult to cater to her needs whilst keeping her safe and protected at all times Andromeda knew she had had to make the decision with a heavy heart but knowing that her daughter was happy and thriving in her new home gave her great comfort and solace.

Things at home had become untenable especially for Cynthia who was greatly distressed and triggered by the fallout from her brother's escapades. Like a slow moving deadly disease infecting all the occupants of the household Elijah's tantrums and adolescent behaviour had destroyed any peace or sanctity in their home Not a day went by without quarrels, arguments fight It had become a toxic space for the girls and Andromeda. No-one could get through to him for love or money He was unaware of the effect it was having on them all.

Letting out a huge sigh of relief, Andromeda put down the receiver. A visitation from social services had been arranged and the process for looking at suitable placements had been put into motion for Cynthia It would not be long now as soon as something came up Cynthia could move into her new place and hopefully she would like it there Andromeda hoped She would also make sure that she could visit her daughter frequently so that the contact between them remained unbroken she vowed to herself. It was for the best and better for her daughter's future she told herself. Their home situation at present was less than ideal for a young adult on the autism spectrum. Until Andromeda eventually got herself sorted and things improved, she could rest in the knowledge that her daughter was in good hands.

She had won one war but the battle was far from over yet. There was still the small matter of Elijah.

CHAPTER 89

GIRLS MOVE OUT

Andromeda's other daughter Mariah who had always been the most studious and diligent of Andromeda's children like her older brother Samuel who studied overseas. She had been offered a place at one the universities of her choice. Both Andromeda and her Mariah had visited quite a few in the last weeks following her school leaving. It turned out that her admission to Liverpool University had been accepted for the Textile and Design course she had wanted.

Mariah had always nurtured a sense for fashion and latest trends, aspiring to create her own collection one day. She was thrilled to receive a place and could not wait to get there. Some of her friends were also going there although they were all doing different courses, but she felt comforted knowing they would be together at least. There would be classes, and parties and so many things going on in the campus, it was an altogether different life living in student accommodation and far away from home. It seemed so exciting. She loved her mother very much, but life at home had become almost unbearable and strained thanks in no little part to her younger brother.

It was awful to watch Elijah put their mother through so much grief, as she struggled to keep their family going. His reckless attitude towards everyone and the daily trouble he brought to their door had rendered living at home a nightmare. Mariah could not wait to get away fast enough. She empathised with mother but she had noticed that their younger sibling received a lion's share of her attention and focus. She had always been the good child, doing her homework and handing in her assignments on time.

There had not been a single complaint from school and her grades had reflected that. She worked hard and kept her head down even when things at home had been tumultuous and chaotic. At least with her, mother had had one less child to worry about. She missed her dad and not a moment went by when she did not think about him. Somehow in the chaos of family life and all her mother's attention diverted to steering her brother away from trouble, she had felt ignored and unacknowledged.

She knew her mother loved them all and did her best to make them happy and feel loved, yet Elijah had robbed them all of their mother's focus in the last few years. He danced rings around her and it angered Mariah but she knew it was hopeless. Mother did have a soft spot for her son because he was the youngest. That much was apparent. It was not fair, she thought scornfully. They all deserved the same, why was he so special, she thought angrily.

Mariah worried about mother once she had left home for university, she hoped that things would settle down for her, as it would only be her brother and mother living at home Surely he would reign in his antics and be more supportive for their mother. She was not getting any younger, and her health had begun to decline due to the stress he had put her under. She was the only parent they had left and Mariah hoped and prayed that Elijah would behave himself and begin to start growing up.

In September, she would begin classes. It was April now, so they had enough time to plan the move and buy the things she needed for her student flat. She was excited and could not wait. Cynthia had also been allocated a date which would be in next month on the 23rd.

It was a lovely detached house nestled upon a hill high up in the lush green valley of Colne It was only a 30 minute drive for Andromeda to drive to and visit her daughter whenever she wanted. Cynthia would be sharing the house with 3 other girls with different learning disabilities, monitored and managed by a staff and a team of support assistants throughout.

Andromeda felt a surge of pain and emotion well up at the thought of her two daughters no longer living at home with her.

The time which she had dreaded all along had arrived all too soon, much to her dismay .They were finally leaving the nest, the home they had lived in for years under the same roof, growing , evolving , more importantly being together as a family.

She had always known this was bound to happen but had never been prepared for. Everything had happened so fast, but Andromeda had known that when the day finally arrived she would be shedding so many tears at parting from her girls. She had read about the empty nest syndrome somewhere but up until now she had not realised it would be so painful.

In part she was relieved for her daughter Cynthia. The help could not have come soon enough. Things had long been spiralling out of control. Her siblings could not cope with a sister who was averse to uncontrollable urges that led to violent and aggressive behaviour both in the home and outside.

Andromeda had needed intervention and the help external agencies to contain the risk that her daughter was susceptible too. Still the house would seem so empty without both her girls and already she could feel the hollow of their absence deepen as the days drew closer.

* * *

EPILOGUE

Looking back now, it had all seemed to be a blur of events, traumas, long fought battles, parental conflicts, but she had come out of them eventually with only a few scars to show for her experiences.

Age and hardship had not only refined her but remoulded her into a different woman. A woman who was now learning to navigate the waters of uncertainty and learn to fend for herself and for her children. She was now in survival mode. All her protective instincts were at the fore propelling her forward with a newfound confidence she was unfamiliar with.

Her husband had made a solemn promise before he had embarked on his trip, vowing that he would take them all to Europe. A road trip, creating memories along the way, visiting cosmopolitan cities, she had never seen before. Only he would never know that he was the one who would going on a solitary one way trip, leaving behind his loved ones, to grieve and mourn his sudden absence.

As the years sped past, Andromeda felt she was now at that stage of life where she had to gradually ease away and succumb to the inevitable fact that her good years as fraught with difficulties as they had been, were now long behind her. It was time to accept that her children were all grown up and responsible for their lives, their decisions, and consequences of their actions.

Having thought that, even adult children were always in need of parental help, despite their newfound independence and individual lives. She let out a sigh as she thought, problems did not dissipate once children flew the nest, and they only got bigger in time and more complex.

She would continue to be that loving presence in all their lives. She had every faith in them and would continue to pray for their health, their joys and successes going forward.

Life in all its unpredictable forms would continue to throw up innumerable challenges every so often as it was inclined to do. Life was never meant to be easy, Andromeda knew from experience, happiness could be as fleeting as sadness only she knew that she would never forget. The searing imprints of past traumas, the numerous trials and loss would be forever etched upon on her mind. She was now much older and calmer as the furious tides of her past began to ebb and flow in unison.

Despite herself, Andromeda felt a renewed sense of visor and hope flowed through her veins as she leaned back against the wall cradling a cup of coffee in both her hands, with a sigh of satisfaction, escaped her lips. "They were going to be ok".

Against many insurmountable odds she had driven a wedge through those belief systems of old, disseminating barriers erected by her relatives and family members. It had been a David versus Goliath undertaking to crush the belly of the beast. The beast which had fed upon greed, corruption, exploitation of vulnerable women.

Single woman and lowly widows were a target for men with predatory nocturnal impulses, waiting in the shadows to pounce and exploit, women like Andromeda.

Andromeda's experiences had shown her that men perceived them as hapless, helpless creatures who could not function without a man to carry the load and burdens which daily life brought. Women in her culture group were deemed to be incompetent, fragile and lacked the intelligence to take any progressive action on their own merit. It was a highly sexist and patriarchal mindset.

Those that did dare to break the mould and bring a voice to the table, only brought suffering upon themselves, from disgruntled, husbands and in-laws.

Whilst she had managed to break through the maze of bureaucratic red tape, and manage her affairs without the help a man by her side, this included sorting her pension, organising her finances and a place to live, she came under fire from many of her husband's colleagues.

Watching her struggle unfold, they had relished in her misery, openly scoffing and mocking her for, working like a man, running around and doing the things that normally her husband would have taken care of.

It was hardly surprising, given the mind-set that prevailed. These men were the typical narrow-minded misogynists who preached that a women's place was in the home, and, venturing outside the confines of her house without a chaperone, invited only slander and trouble although they had no qualms about besmirching Andromeda's character at every available opportunity they got. She could not win either way.

The fact that widows or single women could not be perceived as enterprising, and capable, just as men disgusted Andromeda.

So, what were women like herself supposed to do? Sit it out and starve? Andromeda's thoughts darkened with anger at the audacity of their claims.

She went about her business with a new-found confidence and refused to let their biting comments unsettle her. Despite the many upheavals that came on her path, Andromeda managed to work her way through the mountain of paperwork and formalities required to settle her late husband's matters. Naturally his possessions and share of the estate transferred automatically to his heirs. This evidently had not gone down too well with her in laws. It had only inflamed their outright sense of indignation, upending their nefarious schemes and plans to stake their claims, whilst she was locked in a void of grief.

There was not much that men could do which women could not, and she was more than willing to challenge and prove that's she was as good as any man if not better.
As a widow she had been sentenced by society and her own brethren sadly, to a life of solitude and abandonment. She felt like a ghost who flitted about silently, in the shadows, moving unnoticed amongst the throng as an invisible entity.

There was a time when she had simply ceased to exist to others. Now she felt the rebirth of a new woman, one who was in control of her actions this time.

Her mind had alluded to their judgements, time and time again, convincing her that she was the culprit, the protagonist of all the bad things that befell the family. In actual fact her mind had long since abandoned her and rallied with her adversaries. She was by default, naive and trusting and very sensitive to criticism.

The constant barrage of verbal and mental abuse she had had to endure on a daily basis had eventually worn her down, shredding her nerves and having a detrimental impact on her emotional and psychological state.

Her self-esteem was already in tatters, her confidence had been stripped away layer by layer over the years amounting to a timid, under confident creature in its stead. Her mind was wreaking havoc, day and night with no let up. It compelled her to believe that she enabled the behaviours of others, for she was weak, unintelligent, unattractive and expendable. The mind had literally developed a mind of its own (pun unintended).

It would take years of unlearning all her conditioned learning. To erase the negative assumptions and cut herself some slack.

Andromeda knew one day she would discover who she really was as a person. They had all but broken and shattered every tiny molecule. It was time to draw the line. She knew who she was and that was enough.

She was not a stigma, she told herself repeatedly in her head. These people were the ones with the disease in their minds, where negative beliefs prevailed. She was a free spirit, an entity with free will. Unless she learnt to respect herself, no-one else would.

Her faith embodied the importance and treatment towards women in her situation. Sadly, however, it was not the case in real life. For it seemed to be a direct contrast to the way she was being treated by those from her culture.

Nowhere had it ever been written that women were inferior to men. It was intricately woven in the fabric of society by ancient unbending traditions passed down in feudal, landowning families where Patriarchy was the rule of thumb as far as Andromeda's family was concerned.

No one was going to dictate or tell her what to do and how she should do it.

Andromeda had been dictated to all her life, her wings clipped from an early age. Her thoughts, her persona, her inner creativity, suppressed over the years by these long-entrenched age-old beliefs.

She had broken free or fate had set her free, and she found she could fly after all. She had a voice, she was a person, filled with a zest for life and now it was time to start living for herself and watching her children soar to great heights of success.

Andromeda's legacy would be much different. She vowed with steely determination that she would ensure that her daughters, and granddaughters, were equipped in life to deal with unforeseen circumstances, and able to stand other own merit, and support themselves, to be educated and well versed in all manner of practical and academic life.

Andromeda's widowed status was no longer of any consequence, the label was there by fact but she was still a woman in her own right - a mother, a daughter, a, sister, a friend and there was no longer room in her life for stigma and self-doubt. They had tried and failed. She had managed to beat her demons and those that had once cast her aside and tarnished her name. Experience had taught her in the hardest way possible to learn to respect herself and not be swayed by other people's opinions of her. She had to be brutally determined in order to make a place for herself, in society.

She had begun to flourish again. She discovered bits of herself from the knowledge that she could do many things herself without the cloak of dependency she once lived under.

The realisation that she was able to communicate effectively and make new friends gave her a tremendous boost to her once bruised morale. She rediscovered the person who had long been buried under layers of criticism, and guilt and hatred, the latter of which was mostly self-generated. She had always hated her inability to fight back, or defend against herself against the injustices and blows that had mercilessly been hurled at her.

Those years had cost her a lot in terms of stress, for many reasons, affecting her psychologically and mentally. She had been a neurotic mess for the most part of her life there, worsened by the treatment of her in-laws and the total apathy of her husband towards her plight.

It was an unspoken stigma to go for counselling or therapy in those days. In patriarchal families as Andromeda's, women were mere chattels and home makers, there was no place or patience for women with emotional needs or mental issues. Women were expected to absorb all manner of pain and suffering and hardship without complaint in addition to conforming to the wily expectations which only a patriarchal society could place upon them.

Marriage had taken the best years of her life and with it, infinite amounts of energy.

Raising her four children without a father, one with learning difficulties, and the youngest with profound behavioural issues, had been an insurmountable task. A task made more difficult especially when only one half of two parents existed. Maybe things would have been so much different, had the commanding, presence of their father been alive. Maybe her son would not have derailed as he did, in fact, life would have been so much easier with her husband knowing what to do and how to handle the difficult situations.

Together they would have helped steer their children to safer shores, helped them navigate their way through the choppy waters of life, share in their turmoil, their troubles and supporting them wherever they could. Like beacons of hope and order they would have guided them through along life's treacherous path. Up until now, Andromeda had leant heavily upon her husband for support and left all matters to him, basking in the warm glow and assuredness of his protection. He had been her security blanket and a protective canopy for her children. How was she going to manage without him by her side? A sharp stab of pain and longing seared through her body, at the harsh reality life had dealt her.

Parents could only do their best until their children reached the adult stage, after which they were solely responsible for their own decisions there on. It was the early developmental years of their childhood and early adolescent years that was going to shape, them, make them or break them. Against all odds, Andromeda had survived a forced marriage, widowhood, and the challenges of standing now upon the threshold of time, sparing a brief glance back in her past, Andromeda now looked to the future. She had been handed a second chance and it was now up to her to take back the power and recharge. She would eventually heal from her scars and decades of siphoning her energy into to others. Hopefully now she would focus upon her children and herself It was time to move on and leave the past behind.

2023

She gazed down into the adoring large brown eyes, like two melting pots of chocolate of her 3-year-old grandson and felt a rush of love wash over her like nothing she could describe. This was her progeny, the next generation to succeed her. Despite all that she had encountered in her life to get to this point, the untold hardships and compromises she had had to make, here she was holding in her arms one of life's greatest accomplishments, the sweet innocent child whose smile melted her heart, and filled her with a love so encompassing, that she felt a flood of joyous tears fill her eyes .This would be her legacy, her beautiful grandchildren who would continue her name. Holding her grandson brought home to her how blessed she was. What more could she ask for?

It was hard to fathom how far she had come, beating the stigma and reinventing herself all over again. It was time to say goodbye to the past and look to the future, and relish the beginning of a new dawn, a new era. Every generation that would come and had already arrived learnt from the mistakes of its predecessors. Mistakes that hopefully would never be repeated , girls would be given opportunities that presented themselves , the chance to complete their education , to learn and advance in a variety of life skills , to have the autonomy to choose their own paths ,enable themselves to become fully independent and functioning both within society and their own families. She wanted women to feel empowered and free from the harsh constraints that a patriarchal community placed upon them. Given the tools and encouragement to progress as men were warrant to have, were guarantees to unlimited success in her opinion.

Above all Andromeda hoped for a better future for all women like herself who could walk proudly and with their heads held high, without being stigmatised , and view as unworthy objects when life dealt a cruel blow, for it was life itself that was the real test .The greatest enemy of man was man or woman themselves . Andromeda's journey had been one of her biggest challenges, struggling to survive as a widow and single mom, grappling with the mindset of those who viewed women as little more than helpless and of little worth.

She still had a lot to do, by no means was her journey quite over. Raising her children had been no easy feat, with untold complications along the way. She had nothing to prove or validation to be gotten, from any quarter. Much time had passed, and now she had to trust and believe in herself and make the most of the life she had left by living it doing the things she loved the most.

"It was her time now!"

SEQUEL

The Troubled Son

"It's the Police here, open up, we need you to accompany us to the police station, right away"

"Your son has been taken into custody."

"I have my concerns about where this boy is headed," the grave headmaster said indicating the boy who had upended the entire school with his destructive behaviour.

"That boy is on a trajectory to self-destruct. I do not think he can be helped. He is his own worst enemy. I am extremely worried for him," said Mr. Graham, the head teacher.

All she could do, was watch helplessly as her son descended into a void enmeshed in the iron clad grip of his spiralling addiction. Andromeda braced herself, for there could only be one outcome, she thought grimly and she had to do all she could to prevent that Caught up in the eye of the storm in which all the escape routes had been closed off, there had to be a way, to get through to her son. Oblivious to the carnage and destruction he was leaving in his wake, the boy was slipping through her fingers and free falling into the abyss below.

She knew she was grasping at straws. With no end in sight, Elijah was at war with himself and the world could simply go to hell, for all he cared.

Milton Keynes UK
Ingram Content Group UK Ltd.
UKHW022120091224
452185UK00010B/448